Deadly Secrets

NY State Trooper Series

Jen Talty

Jupiter Press

Deadly Secrets: New York State Troopers Series, Book three

Publishing History
Cool Gus Publishing, 2015

Deadly Secrets

New York State Trooper Series Book Three

USA Today Bestselling Author
JEN TALTY

Praise for Jen Talty

"*Deadly Secrets* is the best of romance and suspense in one hot read!" *NYT Bestselling Author Jennifer Probst*

"A charming setting and a steamy couple heat up the pages in a suspenseful story I couldn't put down!" *NY Times and USA today Bestselling Author Donna Grant*

"Jen Talty's books will grab your attention and pull you into a world of relatable characters, strong personalities, humor, and believable storylines. You'll laugh, you'll cry, and you'll rush to get the next book she releases!" Natalie Ann USA Today Bestselling Author

"I positively loved *In Two Weeks*, and highly recommend it. The writing is wonderful, the story is fantastic, and the characters will keep you coming back for more. I can't wait to get my hands on future installments of the NYS Troopers series." *Long and Short Reviews*

"*In Two Weeks* hooks the reader from page one. This is a fast paced story where the development of the romance grabs you emotionally and the suspense keeps you sitting on the edge of your chair. Great characters, great writing, and a believable plot that can be a warning to all of us." *Desiree Holt, USA Today Bestseller*

"*Dark Water* delivers an engaging portrait of wounded hearts as the memorable characters take you on a healing journey of love. A mysterious death brings danger and intrigue into the drama, while sultry passions brew into a believable plot that melts the reader's heart. Jen Talty pens an entertaining romance that grips the heart as the colorful and dangerous story unfolds into a chilling ending." *Night Owl Reviews*

"This is not the typical love story, nor is it the typical mystery. The characters are well rounded and interesting." *You Gotta Read Reviews*

"*Murder in Paradise Bay* is a fast-paced romantic thriller with plenty of twists and turns to keep you guessing until the end. You won't want to miss this one..." *USA Today bestselling author Janice Maynard*

*First, to my friend Laura Benedict. Without your support,
this book would have never seen publication.
To Wendy S. Marcus, for your support and encouraging
words.
And to Jennifer Probst. You always make me smile.*

Chapter One

Patty Harmon checked the time on her cell phone as a new client left the law offices of Winston and Associates, followed by an entourage of men in very expensive suits, including her boss and his two junior associates. It was only four in the afternoon, but considering this particular client had his own driver, as she noted from her picture window, she figured whatever the man wanted, he got. She squinted, trying to see if the drivers in the two large SUVs had those wiry things attached to their ears, but she couldn't see that far.

Winston and Associates was a small law firm dealing mostly with estates, wills, a few local businesses, and the various needs of some of the locals.

Lately, however, there seemed to be a wave of new clients. Rich clients. Out-of-town clients.

"Hey, Matt," she yelled.

"What's up?" The other paralegal in the office stepped into his doorway, down the hall from hers. She had a view, while he hadn't a single window, but a view of the parking lot wasn't much to talk about, and his office was twice in size, with plush office furniture compared to her metal desk. Matt's office also came with a large bookshelf with all the office resources at his fingertips. When Conrad had hired her, he told her the cushiness of her office was proportional to how much she proved her worth.

"Who's the new big shot?"

Matt was in his mid to late-forties, nice-looking, with short brown hair graying at the temples, and brown eyes. He'd been with Conrad for about nine years before she came on a year ago, and he got the bigger cases. Hell, half her work came from him, not Conrad.

"Keith Holland of Holland Development. They won the bid for the Casino and are looking into putting it on the old Kendrick Paper Company site." Matt leaned against the doorjamb, arms crossed. He always wore khaki pants and a well-pressed dress shirt. If it weren't for the fact he was gay, and she was, well…she couldn't really call herself involved anymore. Reese had made it clear he was never going to settle down. He'd proved that when she broke up with him two weeks ago, and he shrugged and said, "Well, it was fun while it lasted." He then kissed her cheek and walked away, telling her he'd always care. She thought he'd argue with her, asking her not to call it off, expressing his devotion to her. Begging her. Yeah, that was a nice fantasy.

But the reality was, Reese wasn't the marrying type. She had noticed a hint of sadness in his eyes. She knew that look. She knew he cared. But he was closed off. Unable to commit. She couldn't change him.

Nor did she try. Her father had made that mistake, and Patty had ended up paying a huge price for it.

She bit back a sob pushing against her throat. Her life had been so planned. It was going to take some time to get over Reese. She should have listened to her cousin when he'd warned her last summer. Then again, if she had listened, she wouldn't be pregnant.

She dreaded telling Reese he was going to be a father. She could picture the conversation, and it wasn't pretty. He'd likely accuse her of trapping him.

Well, this was no trap. He could be part of his child's life or not, but she was going to have this baby.

"I still can't believe we're going have a casino here in a few years," she said, pulling herself from a train of thought that could only end with her short of a panic attack.

"Well, Holland plans on making this his home away from home. He's looking for other properties to buy, a place he can bring his family and extended family for the summer. I guess he's got a bunch of kids and cousins, all wanting to summer somewhere around here. Seems weird if you ask me."

"Which properties?" Patty asked, intrigued.

"Haven't been told yet," Matt said. "I had him pegged for a 'summer in Saratoga' than in Lake George, but what do I know? Me and rich people, not a good match."

She was about to ask why Holland hired Conrad when she heard the familiar sound of a rifle being cocked.

Matt whipped around. A stranger stood in the hallway with a rifle in his hands. "What the—"

Patty sat frozen in her chair, her hands pressed so hard on the desk they turned white. Matt reached for the rifle, but the stranger holding it was too quick.

Instinctively, she hit the floor and rolled under

her desk. The rifle went off, and Matt let out a blood curdling scream. She closed her eyes and covered her ears. She'd learned that agony firsthand when she'd been shot in the shoulder last summer. Footsteps echoed, and she felt the floorboards vibrate. *Oh, God,* she thought, *what happened to Angela?* If the receptionist had been shot, Patty would have heard it, so where could she be?

"Come out," the stranger said.

Her entire body trembled. She pulled her knees tight to her chest to stop it, but failed. The stranger rounded the desk, then kicked her leg. She looked up, and once again, she was staring down the wrong end of a rifle.

"Get up." His voice was eerily calm. His finger rested over the trigger.

She did as she was told, though not gracefully. Her stomach twisted and tightened so badly she knew she would be sick at any moment. She held her hands high, leaning against the desk for support. She glanced at Matt, who held his knee with both hands, his lips formed into a tight thin line, his pupils dilated from the pain, but he managed to give her a reassuring look. Him not being mortally wounded didn't make her feel better at all.

"Where's Conrad?" the stranger asked.

"I don't know," she said. "He left a few minutes ago, and I don't know where he was going."

"What about you?" The stranger turned his attention to Matt, who had one hand on his bloody knee, while the other reached for his phone, which must have fallen out of his pocket during the short struggle. "I wouldn't do that if I were you, or I'll put a bullet between this pretty woman's eyes."

Matt wrapped both hands around his knee as he fell against the wall, his lips still pursed, his eyelids drooping with defeat.

"Can I tie a belt or something around my friend's leg? He's bleeding something awful." Tears burned a path down her check as she sucked in her breath. "Please," she begged.

The stranger pointed the gun directly at Matt. "Are you wearing a belt?"

Matt nodded.

"All right then," the stranger said. "You can help him with the belt as soon as you get me Conrad on the line."

The stranger kicked Matt's phone toward Patty. "Well, little lady," he said, "you hurry up and make that call if you want to help your friend here with that belt."

Patty's body trembled as if she were the center of an earthquake.

"Are you deaf? Either pick up the phone on your desk or the cell off the floor and call your boss. Tell him Terry is waiting for him, and he better haul ass back to his office and deal with me and no funny stuff or I will kill you."

Patty looked at the phone on her desk for a long moment, then reached for it with a trembling hand. Her other hand pressed protectively over her stomach. The baby was so tiny that it was probably too early to pick up a heartbeat, but she knew it grew inside her. Boy or girl, didn't matter. All she wanted was a chance to have a healthy child.

And the opportunity to tell Reese, no matter his reaction.

"Hurry up, or I'll shoot this guy in the chest." The stranger now pointed the gun at Matt, who grappled with his belt, trying desperately to make his own tourniquet.

"I'm calling him... please don't shoot anyone." Patty gripped the phone with one hand while she braced herself against the desk, shaking so badly she dropped the receiver three times before she was able to bring it to her ear and then dial star one on the phone.

She called Conrad, but it went straight to voice-mail, so she left the gunman's message, then ended the call. She thought about screaming, *He's got a gun, he's shot Matt!* But she figured the stranger would shoot her.

She did not want to get shot today.

"At least let me tend to Matt. He's bleeding too much."

"Go ahead," the gunman said.

Quickly, she knelt beside Matt, taking the belt from his weak hands and tightening it as hard as she could. She locked gazes with Matt, who conveyed an understanding of the situation. There was nothing they could do but sit and wait. And pray.

"Go sit down over there." The gunman pointed to her office chair.

"Please, can I—"

"Whatever it is, no. Now go sit."

Patty did as instructed.

Poor Angela. The gunman must have done something dreadful to her. A flash of the gunman twisting Angela's neck until it snapped raced through her mind's eye. She swallowed, feeling bile rise in her throat.

For the second time in a year, Patty could see the most important parts of her life as if she were thumbing through an old photo album. She had no regrets. Not even Reese, the untamable man, as she had started calling him, but only to herself. It saddened her that he was so emotionally closed off, because deep down he was caring and generous, but he avoided emotions, a master at redirection.

Her only regret was for the baby. It hurt to think this was how both their lives would end.

The tears came on fast. She blinked past them, but she could have sworn she saw Reese running across the hallway. Couldn't be. Could it? Could he have somehow sensed she needed him? That she… that his… no. She was delusional with fear.

The gunman turned toward the hallway. "Anyone else in the office?"

She immediately thought of Angela, but if she'd been here, he would have seen her in the reception area. She shivered at the thought of what fate may have been bestowed on the receptionist. She heard… or maybe felt the old floorboards creak. Her pulse did double time as a shadow emerged.

"Put down your weapon," a familiar voice shouted.

She held her breath. Reese was here. He was actually here. Her heart lifted a little, but she knew this wasn't over as she still stared at the wrong end of a rifle.

"The building is surrounded," came another voice. "Put down your weapon."

"You're going to have to shoot me before I do that, but if you do, my trigger finger will go off, and that nice little lady over there—"

Bang!

The gunman lunged forward as a second shot rang out, shattering the picture window. Patty dropped to the floor, covering her face, and screamed as either a bullet or a piece of glass tore into her calf. She curled up in a ball and rolled back under her desk, seeking any kind of safety from the line of fire.

Under the ringing in her ears, she heard muffled voices, a couple she recognized, and a few new ones. Sirens screeched in the background. Her calf felt as though someone had stuck a knife into it and twisted it. She reached down to feel her leg just as she saw two boots in the opening of the desk. "Who's there?" she whispered, retreating further, pinning herself tightly in the corner.

"Reese." His voice was soft and sweet in her ears. She dropped her head to her knees and began to sob.

"Hey, now, it's okay."

She felt Reese's fingers glide on her leg, then gently

place something around her calf. Even though she knew the situation was under control, the fear didn't leave her body. She flung her arms around Reese, banging her head on the desk, but she didn't care. To be in his arms was the only way she was going to feel safe.

"I can't have you moving, okay?" Reese cupped her face, tilting her head. His blue eyes were so warm and caring. She could get lost in those deep orbs. "You've got a pretty nasty cut, so until the EMTs arrive, you stay put, okay?"

She nodded.

He wrapped his arms around her, holding her close, making her feel safe, making her feel tingles she'd tried to forget just two short weeks ago. This was not going to be an easy man to get over. Her body shook even more.

"You're going to be okay," he said. "Trust me."

She wanted so wanted so badly to tell him about the baby. While the fear for her life was past, the fear that something might have happened... Before she could finish her thought, she emptied the contents of her stomach all over Reese's New York State Trooper uniform.

"Not the kind of greeting I anticipated." He took a towel a young female trooper tossed his way and wiped Patty's lips, face, and clothing, ignoring his own need to clean off. "Want some water?"

She shook her head as she stared up at his blue eyes, offset by his naturally darker Italian complexion. His hair was jet-black, and he wore the same jarhead haircut as that of half her male family members.

But it looked so much better on Reese.

Everything looked better on Reese.

"I'm so sorry," she mumbled, but she couldn't let go of him. She hugged him tighter, trying to make the trembling in her body stop.

"It's okay," he said. "You're going to be just fine." His voice was so deep, so incredibly calming. His right hand stroked her hair, and his left danced across her arm. "Ambulances should be here any moment." His eyes fluttered, like butterfly kisses as he pressed his lips to her temple. "I've got you," he whispered. "You're okay."

"Matt!" Patty cried. "Where's Matt?" She tried to stand, but a sharp pain tore through her calf. Reese gripped her shoulders.

"I don't think you're hurt too bad, but I can't have you moving at all, okay?" He glanced under the towel over her leg. "You've got a piece of glass in your leg. I can't tell how deep it is, so until the EMTs get here, you don't move it. Got it?"

She nodded. "How is Matt?"

"My partner is tending to him, and we're going to make sure he gets the care he needs."

"Frank's here?" Her cousin Frank had introduced her to Reese...and warned her about him.

"He's here, but he's outside. My new partner is Stacey," Reese said. "She's a good cop, but so young. Barely even legal to drink. Makes me feel like an old man."

Patty had always enjoyed Reese's dry sense of humor, but often wondered if it was a defense mechanism. She wrapped the blanket Reese offered around her body while he looked at her leg again. She couldn't bring herself to look down, and he did his best to block her view. "How did you know to come here?"

"Angela," Reese said. "She was in the bathroom when the perp came in. She called 9-1-1."

"I'm so glad she's okay." And Matt was okay. And Reese was okay. Oh, how she missed his touch. His calloused hands against her smooth skin. His full lips pressed against hers, their tongues entwined in a ritualistic dance. He made her feel she was the only person in the room. It might not be real, but being in his arms again made everything else fade away, except one thing.

She couldn't tell him about the baby until she knew for sure things with the pregancy were okay. Considering the day's events, she worried that something might have happened. She also worried how Reese was going to react to the news, so it was best she wait. At least that was what she told herself.

She watched in a daze as the medics arrived. One group tended to Matt, while another buzzed around her like bees on honey. She chose to focus on the tight grip she had on Reese's hand. She couldn't let go. Didn't want to let go. Thankfully, he stood by her side the entire time.

The other group of EMTs rolled Matt out into the parking lot. He was pale but managed a thumbs-up in her direction.

She gripped Reese's hand tighter when she felt him try to pull away. He looked down at her, locking gazes. "Let them put you on the gurney."

"I think we should let the ER doctors pull that out," she heard one of the EMTs say. "Doesn't look too bad, though."

"I'm going to need her statement," Reese said as he helped load her into the ambulance. "I'll be right behind you," he said, cupping her face and pressing his lips against hers. "Hang tight." He stepped out of the ambulance.

"Reese," she called.

He turned. "I'll be right behind you."

She placed her hands over her stomach, closed her eyes. The baby...

Most people considered New York State Trooper Reese McGinn a loner, a role he'd fallen into nicely until he moved to Lake George. His unit was small, making it impossible to avoid human contact, but he managed to keep his distance.

Until he met Patty Harmon.

He knew heartbreak. He wrote the book on it. The breakup with Patty was something entirely different.

He was lonely, for the first time in years.

He was going to have to get over her. He no longer believed in the sanctity of marriage. Been there. Done that. Bought the T-shirt. Lost the T-shirt.

Patty had her life planned out. She knew exactly the kind of man she'd marry and how many kids they would have. It was apparent when they hooked up that Patty knew what she was getting into, and frankly, she was using him for one wild fling because she'd never done anything crazy.

She had also never done anything for herself. She had spent her entire childhood taking care of her parents and everyone else in the Harmon family. She needed to get outside of herself, just once, and he was happy to oblige. She was beyond beautiful. Her eyes were the most welcoming soft brown he'd ever seen. Her light complexion blended perfectly against her short mousy-brown hair, with just enough thickness to make running his hands through it a daily experience. Stroking her hair as they wheeled her toward the ambulance had been bittersweet.

He never anticipated that he'd grow to care for her beyond the line he'd so carefully drawn for himself. He found himself longing to go for walks and to tell her about himself and to listen to her talk about anything. He kept telling himself it was because she never tried to change him. There were no ties with her, and it actually came as a shock that she'd been the one to call it quits. He'd been so stunned he couldn't muster up a decent response.

She broke up with him, and he put in his transfer papers. He sold himself on the idea he'd been in

Lake George long enough, and it was time to move on.

Seeing Patty, held at gunpoint, had forced him to start second-guessing his current plans. He'd spent the last seven years bitter and angry until he came to this place. Dating Patty had made him never want to leave.

He glanced at the sun, then back at his feet, and started to pace by his truck in front of Patty's duplex; the combination of wet snow and the softened ground underneath made for a muddy path. The winters in Lake George, New York, were brutal, including the month of April, but they were at least on the upswing, and any snow that fell wouldn't stick long. He took in a slow breath, doing his best to keep his pulse from causing him a heart attack. Only two women had ever made him nervous.

One was dead.

The other he hadn't seen in seven years.

Now he could add a third. Patty made him nervous in an entirely new way. He felt like a school-boy, asking his best buddy to ask some girl to be his girlfriend.

Patty seemed to come back with a resounding no. Yesterday, at the hospital after her statement, she'd done everything but drop-kick him out of the hospital room. It was obvious she wanted him gone. So why had she demanded he come over tonight, saying they *really* needed to talk?

His ex-partner, Frank, lived in the other side of the duplex. Frank's car was nowhere to be found, although his wife, Lacy, was probably looking out the window.

A tiny bit of snow remained on the stairs from the last flurry, so Reese grabbed the shovel and cleared it away, the gesture unnecessary except to stall for time.

Frank's door flew open.

"Hey, Reese," said Andy, Lacy's nephew. "Whatcha doing here?" Andy was a good boy who'd been through his share of shit in his short life. Andy's father had murdered his mother and tried to have Andy and Lacy killed. The boy seemed to be bouncing back, thanks to Lacy and Frank and the rest of the Harmons. They were good people. Just what a young boy needed to become a grown man capable of everything Reese was not.

"Came to talk to Patty," Reese said, giving the boy a good shoulder squeeze. "How goes things with you?"

"Other than I'm failing science, good."

"I was always good in science. Let me know if I can help. You still got my number?"

"I do."

"Text me anytime."

Patty opened the door to the upstairs apartment, then smiled at Andy and Reese. Her smile had always been so genuine, but this time it faded quickly. "Come on up," she said.

It saddened Reese that seeing him would bring her to a frown. He took the steps slowly, shedding his boots and coat at the top before entering the one-bedroom apartment that he had frequented just a few weeks ago. Their fling had lasted nearly eight months, the longest he'd had in seven years.

And the only fling he didn't want to end.

Patty wore a pair of sweatpants that hugged her round ass like a glove. The sweatshirt, however, was three sizes too big. Her short brown hair was styled and pushed behind her ears. It looked as if she were trying to grow it out. He'd always liked her short hair, but he also thought a few inches longer, maybe falling just short of her shoulders would be perfect.

As he entered her apartment, he wondered what her response would be if he asked her about starting over.

He swallowed. Never in a million years did he

think another woman could make him feel so much. He'd fought it so hard when it came to Patty, and it shouldn't have surprised him when she dumped him. It had only been two weeks, but she seemed like she couldn't care less that they were over.

He, on the other hand, could barely hold it together. Putting in for that transfer had made him feel sick, but he didn't know what else to do.

"I swear that boy grew an inch just in the last month," he said, falling back on small talk.

"His voice is getting deeper too," she said.

Reese nodded. "Frank really loves that boy."

"I know he does," Patty said. "Thankfully, Andy's father gave up parental rights."

"His father is in prison," Reese said, "for trying to kill the boy. I would certainly hope his rights were stripped away."

"Frank and Lacy are filing for adoption."

"That's great," Reese said. Frank wouldn't up and leave Andy like his biological father had. It saddened Reese that Andy had to know the ugly truth about his old man, but, Reese believed it was better than not knowing your father altogether.

"Can I get you a drink?"

"How about a cup of hot chocolate?"

"That I can do," she said. "Why don't we sit in

the family room?"

He stood in the middle of the small room and contemplated where to sit. The chair, so he could see her beautiful figure outlined in the moonlight glowing over the lake? Or the sofa, where he could feel the heat coming from her body?

He chose the chair, a safer distance.

From the chair, he could see out the window. The lake was no longer a frozen tundra, but he suspected the water felt like a freezer box, even though they were only weeks away from putting the patrol boats in. He had often thought about putting down roots here, but roots were not his strong suit.

"Thanks." He took the mug she offered and blew on the liquid, then sipped it before placing the mug on the coaster. Patty was big on coasters. A habit he'd acquired and would probably take with him to his next place of employment. "How are you doing today? You don't seem to be limping too badly."

"Doesn't hurt so much, but it's been a long twenty-four hours." She sat on the sofa, tucking her good leg under her, and sipped her cocoa. "Thank you," she said. "I can't imagine it was an easy thing to do…to kill a man."

"I did my job." He continued to stare out the window instead of at her. He drew in a long, deep breath. Reese McGinn, the emotionally unavailable man, a pile of emotions who could barely form two words together.

They grew silent. Normally, he enjoyed the quiet. Preferred it. Now, in this moment, watching her long fingers wrap around the mug as she brought it to her perky pink lips, he wished for noise. Anything. The silence made him feel as though he were about to jump out of his skin. He shifted his position three times.

"I just found out a couple of days ago." She changed positions on the sofa, lifting her injured leg up, propping her foot on a pillow. "So I'm trying to get used to the idea..."

"Found out what?"

"No questions. Just let me get through this. Okay?"

He nodded.

"Yesterday made me realize, again, how precious and short life is, and that life doesn't always go as planned."

He stared at her, watching her sip from her mug between words. He had drained his as soon as it cooled, but she took her time. She deserved so much more than he could ever give her. He could be a rock. A pillar of strength. But he wasn't sure he could be a partner, no matter how much he wanted to.

He would hurt her, and he couldn't live with that.

Breaking up wasn't what he wanted, but he had no idea what that meant.

"My childhood was difficult," she continued, "and I promised myself I would do things differently. I thought if I planned everything out, I'd have the perfect little family."

"I'm sure you'll have everything you want."

"Let me finish." She swiped at her cheek.

He moved to the couch, then sat next to her, putting an arm around her. It felt so good just to touch her that he told himself that would be enough. "You've been through a lot. No one deals with facing death the way you have easily, and you need to just go through—"

"I'm pregnant."

"Really, you just..." He heard the words, but his brain was taking a while to decipher the meaning. "What did you just say?"

"I'm pregnant."

"Come again?" He shot up from the couch, then walked to the other side of the room with his mouth hanging open. "Did you just say pregnant? As in a baby?"

She rested her cup on the coaster and caught his gaze. Her eyes filled with a mixture of hurt and fear. His gut tightened as if he'd been sucker punched. She was pregnant. He was going to be a father. The last time a woman uttered those words, he'd been overwhelmed with gratitude...but no sooner did he feel joy than he felt the most agonizing pain he'd ever felt in his life.

A pain he thought he had buried so deep it couldn't resurface, yet here it was, hitting him so deep that all he could see or feel was the rage that had been sieged upon him years ago.

"How?" he asked. "I mean, we always used protect..." Then he remembered. It only took one reckless night. He started to pace in front of the coffee table, as he'd done outside. He ran a hand across his head. His heart swelled with a mixture of fear, anger, joy, and hope. How could one moment in time cause so many conflicting emotions? He had no idea how to respond. How he really felt. He needed time to think. Just as he turned to tell her that, he walked right into the coffee table, dumping the rest of her cocoa all over her lap, turning her sweats into a chocolatey mess.

"Crap, I'm sorry." He stood there, staring at her like a fool.

She looked at him with narrowed eyes. "I need a towel."

He stumbled to the galley kitchen, then grabbed the paper towels. By the time he got back, she'd already gotten a towel from the bathroom.

"At least the sofa is leather, and the floor is hardwood. I need to change." She disappeared into the bedroom while he continued to clean up the mess, trying not to think.

His baby. At one time, he had wanted a child. Then Jessica destroyed everything.

Now? He wasn't entirely sure of anything. He'd been so closed to the idea, he never allowed himself even a fantasy of being a family man.

The last time he'd been told he was going to be a dad he'd only been twenty. What the hell did he know? How could he know his soon-to-be bride would destroy the one thing that gave him hope for a better future than his mother, or the man he called Father, had made for him?

He sank to the floor, not caring about the residual wet seeping into his clothes. He had done his best to forget the final words of his mother before she died, and the secret she took to her grave.

Reese had tried to find his real father but had almost no information. His grandparents didn't help, maintaining they'd always believed Allen McGinn, who was still rotting in prison, was Reese's father. Reese had been seven when Allen was convicted of murder.

He'd been devastated. Allen hadn't been the best father in the world, but he'd tried. The few times he got off drugs, he'd play ball in the yard and take Reese fishing. When he left, Reese was left empty-hearted, with a likewise drug-addicted mother who was incapable of taking care of herself, much less him.

When he was twenty, she died, after telling him the truth about Allen, but never telling him the name of his real father. When asked, she'd said, "You don't want to know. He would have been worse than Allen." She slipped into a deep coma and died three hours later.

"Hey." Patty's voice snapped him out of his trip down not-so-happy memory lane. "Sorry I just blurted that out." She sat down on the other side of the sofa as he eased himself onto the couch as well. "Not how I wanted to tell you."

"You're sure about this?" He'd done the honorable thing with Jessica, and in the end, got his heart ripped out. Patty wasn't Jessica. The two women couldn't be more different. That knowledge did nothing to help him sort through how he really felt. Or what this really meant for him. "How do you feel?"

"I'm a little scared, but physically, I feel fine."

"Everything that happened yesterday? The baby... it's okay?"

She nodded. "I'm not so sure you're okay."

He had to agree. "This is kind of a big deal." He tried to push the negative thoughts out of his head, reminding himself that maybe he was being given a second chance, but a second chance at what? He stood and started pacing again, a nervous habit he'd developed over the years. He tried to stop, but it helped him sort the chaos in his brain.

"It's a very big deal," she said. "Unexpected, but it's a reality."

Fear squeezed his heart so tight he could barely breathe. He needed time. He needed to think. He needed a stronger drink than hot cocoa. "So what do you need from me?" He knew it was a shit thing to say. A cop-out from manning up and doing the right thing, which would have been to beg her to take him back. To get on his hands and knees and tell her he'd do anything to make this work.

Once bitten, twice shy.

"I don't really know," she said calmly. Too calmly,

and that made him even more jittery. "I'm not asking for anything. Your involvement in this baby's life is up to you. I understand you're planning on moving, and that's okay. I'm not asking you to be something you're not."

"But I am going to be a father." He struggled with anger and old fears. He wasn't used to this emotional shit. He'd thought it died the moment Jessica aborted his baby. "We're going to be parents."

She nodded.

He stopped pacing in front of the picture window, put his hands on his hips, and said nothing. A million things rattled his brain, but he just couldn't wrap his mind around the idea that this could really be his reality. A family. Yet she wasn't asking him to be a father. She'd just, and quite flippantly too, stated that his involvement was up to him.

"You okay?"

He found his tongue...sort of. "I'm... I want to be with you. With our baby. I just wasn't...wasn't... Well, it's not what I expected, but..." Why couldn't he just blurt out the words?

"We have time to work out the logistics." She stood and limped toward the door. "I think we both need to let this all sink in." His brain registered that her hand shook as she placed it on the door handle, but he wasn't sure what that meant. She was saying one thing, but her body was telling him something else.

"You want me to leave now?" He managed to shake some of the cobwebs from his brain and organize his thoughts. The breakup. Not wanting to break up, but not being able to commit, or even express he didn't want things to end. Now a baby? A baby that he knew, at the bottom of his heart, with everything he was, he wanted.

And loved.

And she wanted him to leave. *Holy shit*. Did he actually think those thoughts? He'd been torn about the breakup, and then seeing her with a gun to her head, well, he knew then he wanted to get back with her. But a baby? Him a father? "I know I'm not handling this well, but I think we've got a lot to discuss. And plans. We need to make plans. I mean… a baby. That's big deal and we've got—"

"I think you need some time to think about all this." Her words and tone were even. Too even. Patty had never been your stereotypical overly emotional female, but some emotion right now might actually be nice. Instead, he got stoic. A little voice in his head reminded him that she had a tendency to keep her own emotions close to her chest.

"No," he nearly yelled. "We should be talking about where we're going to live and things like that. I mean, we're going to have a baby together."

"We are, but for one, it's not going to happen for a few months, and two, you're going to be living right here. For all I know, you could be in Buffalo this time next year."

"I can't believe you just said that. That you could think I would just walk away." How could she act like it was no big deal, and he could waltz in or out anytime he wanted. That wasn't going to happen. If he was going to be a father, he was damn well going to be a father, hook, line, and sinker. He gave Allen kudos for at least trying. Reese could do more than try. He took in a deep breath, calming his nerves. He didn't want yell at her, though he did want to take her by the arms and either shake her till she came to her senses or… "You can't do this alone."

"Oh, yes, I can," she said as she stood taller. Prouder. As if he'd somehow insulted her intelligence and capabilities. "You've made it clear the entire time I've known you that you're not a family man, and I accept that. I don't want to change you, or trap…" Her words trailed off with a slight tremor.

"A baby changes everything." He reached out and took her hand. Tentatively, she held it for a moment and then pulled it away, clasping her shaking hands together. Her trepidation saddened him. What little emotion she showed through her body terrified him because he was… The way he'd treated her from day one…was the reason she couldn't trust he'd stick around. Do the right thing.

The right thing doesn't always turn out to be the right thing. He was going to have to get that voice out of his head.

"I don't want you to do this out of obligation." Her brown eyes softened as she stared directly into his. "Please, take a day or two and think about all this. Then we can talk. Please? I think we both need it."

"I am the baby's father." Reese took in another long, slow breath, practically counting to ten, but it did nothing to calm his nerves or lower his blood pressure. "It's not fair to keep a child's father from him." Reese ran a shaky hand across his face. His entire body shook. "And I don't think it's fair to keep a father from knowing his child."

"I'm not keeping anything from you," she said, her voice reassuring, but she stood there, holding the door open, waiting for him to leave. "I'm also not forcing it down your throat. I've always accepted who you were, and I respect that. If you want to stick around, then that's really wonderful. I welcome it. I just don't want you making any rash decisions. I've had a couple of days. You…need time."

Her calmness and rationale were going to be the end of his already frazzled nerves. Even if she did make valid points, but he chose to ignore them. "I'm not making any rash decisions. We need to think about living together. Maybe buying a house."

She shook her head. "You're talking crazy."

"You're the one who's talking crazy." How could she be so calm? So calm and strong, as if she knew she could do this all without his help? Or wanted to do this without his help.

As if she believed he'd bail. "That's our baby." He pointed to her stomach. "Yes?"

She nodded.

"Then we're going to be a couple. A family."

"Are you suggesting we get married?"

He cringed. He wasn't opposed, but it was complicated. Too complicated. She had no idea how complicated.

"I didn't think so," Patty said.

"I'm his father." The word *father* echoed in his ears like the drum in a marching band. It was just a word, but as he'd learned once before, words could destroy a man.

Jessica had done exactly that to him.

"I think living together would be a good start." Boy, was that a loaded proposition. He meant it, but the conversation was derailing, and he wasn't helping matters.

"We don't love each other, and I will not be in a loveless relationship, much less a marriage. I saw what that did to my parents, and they did me no favors by staying together as long as they did."

"I'm not asking you to be in a loveless anything." He strode toward her. "We haven't even given ourselves the chance to be anything."

"We both know what this was, and neither of us pretended it to be anything more."

"We have no idea what we could be together," he said.

"I don't need you to be honorable," she said, handing him his boots. "We wouldn't be having this conversation if I weren't pregnant. You'd be doing your thing, and I'd be doing mine."

"I don't know about that," he admitted. "I thought about us getting back together. I thought about it every day for the last two weeks."

"You never told me that," she said. "And resuming a fling isn't the same thing."

"Maybe not, but it would have been a start. You

tell me you're pregnant, and then tell me to leave, without giving me a chance to figure all this out."

"That's why I want you to leave. Give you a chance to figure it all out. You need some time to deal with whatever you're feeling, because frankly, you are all over the map."

Okay, so he did have to give her that. "So are you. You're acting like this doesn't matter at all. No big deal. You're having our baby, but I don't have to do anything."

A single tear rolled down her cheek. "It matters very much. I just don't want you to feel trapped. I don't want you to have any regrets. I want you to spend some time with the idea that I am...that we are, having a baby. I'm not shutting you out. I would never do that. But I can't have 'this' conversation while you're so riled up."

"So, I go think about this for a few days, then we have a discussion about it all."

She nodded.

"Okay," he said. He paused, contemplating kissing her or something, but then opted to heed her advice. He did need time, but not because he needed to think about what he wanted, but more about what he had to do. He went down the stairs, thinking hard. The closer he got to his truck, the more terrified he became. Not about being a father. About being a *good* father. And how could he even begin to try to build any kind of life with Patty when he was still married to Jessica?

He needed a drink.

Chapter Two

Patty hadn't slept well in days. No amount of hemorrhoid cream was going to get rid of the black circles and puffiness under her eyes. Between the shooting and Reese's totally out-of-character behavior, Patty found herself completely off-balance. Her hormones were out of whack to boot.

She wasn't sure how she'd expected Reese to act or what he'd say, but suggesting they live together had not been it. Honestly, she'd envisioned two possible outcomes: the "how dare you try to trap me" scenario, or the "you're on your own, babe" scenario. Not the "I'm going to stick around and be a father, and we're going to be a family" scenario, though she had dreamed of that. That he'd come home from a long day at work, scoop up his baby, and coddle him or her with words of love and admiration. Then, later, when the baby was asleep, he'd whisper in her ear how much she meant and how grateful he was to have her in his life. Maybe he'd even say those three little words that were almost impossible for him to say, and mean it.

It was a nice dream.

That dream scared her the most. Her father had been head over heels in love with her mother. Her mother didn't carry the same torch, but for the sake of family, they got married when Patty came around. Patty had no idea why her mother stayed for almost sixteen years, but one morning, out of the blue, she and her dad woke up, and Mom was gone. She'd left a note: *Can't be a wife and a mother. I was never cut out for the job.* Patty wasn't shocked, and neither was her father, but he'd been devastated. He'd done everything under the sun to try to make his wife happy.

To this day, Patty barely heard from her mother, though Debbie Cantell's Facebook page showed her living large and enjoying every minute of it. Her father spent a decade being drunk and depressed. Only in the recent year had he been trying to clean up his life.

Forcing a child on Reese would only continue the

loveless cycle. All Patty wanted was an honest life. She could handle anything with an honest life.

Patty walked into the local greasy spoon, looking forward to a late breakfast with Lacy. She also looked forward to a big order of their soaked French toast with crispy bacon. What she hadn't looked forward to were the questions from everyone in the restaurant about her experience at gunpoint, and the fact that the smell of grease and bacon made her stomach flip and flop.

"You must have been terrified," the waitress said. "Is it true what they say? That your life flashes before your eyes."

"Not really." Patty didn't feel bad at all about bursting this young girl's fantasy. "But you do think about life."

The waitress frowned, but then followed up with, "Bet you're glad you didn't get shot like that poor other guy."

"I'm not glad anyone got shot," Patty said.

"Can we order?" Lacy interjected.

The waitress frowned again, but took their order and stopped asking questions.

Finally, when their food was brought, people in the restaurant seemed to get the hint that she didn't want to talk about it. "This the best French toast ever." Patty had shoved the bacon to the side, unable to even look at it without feeling as though she might lose her appetite.

"I know," Lacy said. "Every time I come here, I gain five pounds."

"It's not too cold out. We could go for a walk," Patty said.

"Your idea of cold and mine are two different things." Lacy had lived in Vegas, and it had most definitely thinned her blood for the cold, as they say, though April in Lake George could be thirty and snowing, or fifty and sunny. Today it was forty-two and partly sunny, but it was a push in the right direction.

"I saw Reese at your place yesterday. What's up with that?"

"Well, now that's an interesting story." Patty took a few more bites, then pushed aside her plate. "Seems I'm pregnant."

"Holy shit," Lacy said, dropping her fork onto her plate.

Patty nodded.

"And how do you feel about it?"

"I'm scared, but happy." Patty let a smile spread across her face. Even with all the chaos, she was happy.

"How'd Reese take that news?"

"Better than I excepted." She believed, one hundred percent, that he was happy to be a father, but not that he wanted any kind of relationship with her. He didn't seem to understand that being a father didn't mean they had to be a couple.

"Does that mean you're back together?" Lacy used to be a cynic and certainly didn't believe in a happily ever after. A lot has changed over the course of a year.

"We were never really together to begin with, so that would be a no."

"But he didn't run out on you."

The man that left her apartment yesterday wasn't the man she thought she knew. When he'd first come to town, there had been a bit of gossip about him. Patty knew quite a few women who'd tried to bed him with the intent of landing him. They had all failed.

Reese was discreet. Their relationship—and she decided it was something of a relationship—had never been on public display. "Nope. He suggested we move in together."

Lacy laughed. "I'm kind of surprised he didn't offer to marry you. He is the noble type."

"When he said we needed to be a family, I asked

him if he meant marriage. Should have seen the look on his face. It was like I'd kicked him where it counts."

"But does he want to be a father?"

"I believe he does, but he seems to think being a couple is going to make or break a child's happiness."

"And you believe differently?"

Patty nodded. "I don't want to be with a man who only wants to be with me because I'm carrying his child. I can't live my life that way."

"Have you really given him a chance?"

Lacy proposed a valid question, one that Patty wasn't sure she could be totally honest about because she wasn't sure if giving him a chance meant having her heart ripped to shreds, or having her kid's heart broken. The former she could live with. The latter was a deal breaker. "I'm giving him a chance now."

"No," Lacy said. "You've given him the opportunity to run."

"That is not..." Patty knew Lacy was right. Patty had set up the entire conversation so that Reese could walk away and not feel guilty. She let out a long sigh. "When he didn't hightail it out of my apartment, I did tell him to go think about things. That's something of a chance."

"Yeah. A chance to run. It sounds like that is what you want. Or maybe expect and the idea he'd do anything different freaks you out."

"Could you take my side on this?" Patty let out a puff of air.

"I am," Lacy said. "Perhaps it's time for you to take a risk and let him in."

"I don't know if I can do that," Patty admitted.

"I think you owe that to your baby."

Patty wanted a happy, healthy environment for her child. From the second she found out she was pregnant, she loved the baby more than anything in the world. "I don't want my child to feel like I did when my mother ran out. It took years of very expensive therapy to get over that one."

"You have no idea what things will be like in twenty years. If I had continued to live my life with that kind of thinking, I wouldn't be here right now. There are no guarantees in life."

"I understand, but I'm not making the same mistakes my parents made."

"All right," Lacy said. "Tell me. How do you really feel about Reese?"

That was a loaded question, one Patty wasn't

sure she could answer honestly, and not just to Lacy, but to herself. "He's a good man but no one is close to him," Patty said. "I once asked him about his family, and he said he didn't have a family. I asked him what happened, because everyone has parents, and he just shrugged and changed the subject. He's more than a private person. He's downright secretive." That worried Patty more than anything else. Having a child with him, without knowing about all of him, scared Patty. Secrets hurt people. She didn't want her child to be hurt by his or her own father.

"Why didn't you push him to tell you?" Lacy asked.

"Honestly, I didn't want to know. It was supposed to be a fling."

"But you have feelings for him."

She might feel something for Reese, as the father of her baby, but she couldn't risk her heart, or their baby's on a man who not only had secrets, but didn't want to ever have a family to begin with. People don't change that quickly.

If at all.

Reese wondered what was worse, the hangover or waking up in his boss' house, at noon, with no recollection of how he got there.

He opted for the latter, based on Jared's expression at the lunch table.

They didn't speak much while Jared's wife and three children ate their lunches. Reese politely answered questions from Caitlyn, Jared's inquisitive daughter, while distracting the twins, who constantly tried to get Reese's attention and played peek-a-boo with each other. He thanked Ryan, Jared's wife, for her hospitality, then tried to explain hospitality to Caitlyn while his pounding headache continued to wreak havoc on his ability to think straight. Lucky for him, the television in the family room seemed more interesting to the children than the still-drunk man in the kitchen, and they quickly left to watch their favorite movie.

Reese held his head high, though he wanted to drop it in shame. Rarely did he ever drink to the point of no return. Not only did he dislike being out of control, but it brought back certain childhood memories that he would rather forget.

"You need to drink that water," Ryan said. "If you can stomach it, you should really eat that insanely greasy egg, sausage, bacon, and cheese sandwich I made. Instant hangover cure."

"I can attest to that," Jared said. "She used to have to make me those all the time, before we got together."

Reese wanted to ask why, since Jared wasn't the biggest drinker on the planet, but between cotton-mouth and the fear of losing his cookies, he opted for another sip of water, then forced down a small bite of the greasy sandwich. Odd how that worked; it did ease the cramping and gurgling of his intestines, but nothing could ease his mind about the woman that carried his child. He'd acted like a stupid teenager when she'd told him, reverting back into the dark place he'd lived for so long until he took the job as a state trooper and met Patty.

She had changed so much of his life. He thought about other people in a way he hadn't done so in years. The timbre of her laugh made his heart soar. Her smile made it skip a beat. Everything about her made him want to be a better man. Only, he fought it every step of the way. Truth be told, he was still fight-ing. "I'm sorry," he managed. "It was a rough night."

"What do you remember?" Jared asked. He'd pushed his plate aside and was now leaning back in his chair, swirling the cup of hot coffee his wife had poured, acting like some father dealing with a teenager who'd gotten drunk for the first time. "I remember being at the Mason Jug, drinking heavily, but that's about it." Stupid way to react to being a father, but it wasn't being a father that scared him.

Being without Patty was what screwed with his mind. He hadn't been prepared to face that, much less deal with it before being transferred.

Ryan excused herself, then left the kitchen, closing the old-fashioned swinging door to the family room.

"My brother-in-law owns the bar. He called me when you picked a fight with him when he took your car keys."

"I kind of remember that," Reese said, with flushed cheeks. "I wasn't going to drive. I wanted to sleep it off."

"Not the point," Jared said. "He takes it personally when someone, especially one of my troopers, calls him a few choice names."

"I will make sure I apologize," Reese said, trying to recall as many of the evening's events as he could, but most memories came to him in a drugged, dreamlike state, making it impossible for him to trust any single one. "I really have no acceptable excuse."

"The incident at Conrad's office?"

Reese nodded, though that wasn't really the truth, and he wondered if he would have acted differently during the crisis if he'd known about the baby before the kill shot. The baby changed everything.

"That was a tough one, but I suspect the shooting isn't what has you so twisted inside."

Reese took another small bite of the sandwich, keeping his gaze on the plate. Jared was only fifteen years older, tops, but a million years wiser. He was like the old man down the street that knew everything, loved everyone, and was loved by all. A long silence passed. Reese wasn't sure what to say, or how to say it. Jared didn't let him off the hook, either. "Not entirely."

"I know you and Patty were somewhat of an item, but you broke up?" Jared phrased it as a question, as if he didn't know the details, and Reese damn sure knew he did. Jared knew things about people because Jared was in tune with the world around him. A people whisperer. Reese had enjoyed working under Jared, but it was also unnerving. Jared didn't pry often, but when he did, he was always on the mark.

"It's complicated."

"That's a cop-out," Jared said. "And what you did yesterday is more powerful because you care about her."

"Been there. Done that. Bought the T-shirt," Reese said. He knew it was a flippant response, but until he found Jessica and properly divorced her, it was the only response anyone would get. He couldn't expect Patty to start a life with him when he was already married, and he didn't see the point in upsetting her any more, considering all she'd been through. Until he had his ducks in a row, he would take things one step at a time.

That would be an interesting change of pace.

"When your personal life interjects itself on the job, it affects us. That's a reality."

"It is personal, but it's not going to affect how I do my job. How I did my job."

"All right," Jared said. "Is there something you want to ask me?"

"Why do you say that?"

Jared let out a short laugh. "You told me to revoke your transfer last night."

"I don't remember that," Reese admitted, "but can you?"

"I can, but you need to answer me a few curious questions first."

Reese took another bite. This one going down much easier than the last. Ryan had been right about the sandwich. His head no longer pounded and the ache in his stomach subsided. "Ask me anything. I'll answer." He knew he should be opening up to Patty, but this was a start.

"When I picked you up, you were rambling on some crazy shit about your mother and father, and how you don't know who your father was and how unfair that was."

"I guess I was pretty hammered."

"That's putting it mildly," Jared said. "I thought your father was in jail."

"He's not my biological father, according to my mother." Reese pushed his plate aside. He hadn't told anyone about his family in years. He'd been ashamed. Didn't matter it wasn't his fault, but the little boy inside believed everything he touched went to hell in a handbasket, as his mother had told him on numerous occasions. She'd even said his real father wouldn't have wanted him anyway. "Some current events have roused some emotional baggage from childhood."

"Ryan had it really rough as a kid. Her stepfather

beat her mother to death. It's not something you go around talking about with everyone you meet. So I understand. But last night you said how easy it was to fuck up a kid's life without even trying, and no way in hell would you be doing that, and Patty was just going to have to suck it up."

"Oh." Reese didn't remember a thing about that. "What, exactly, did I say?"

Jared leaned forward and stared at him. "You told me Patty was pregnant."

Reese sat in silence, contemplating those words and the shock he still felt. "Probably shouldn't say anything to anyone since I just found out last night and, well…that conversation didn't end well."

"Frank's going to come after you with a shotgun," Jared said. "It won't be loaded, but he'll enjoy watching you sweat."

"You're not funny." Reese knew Frank wasn't going to be upset over the baby, but the marriage? That might be an entirely different story. Reese needed to take care of that right quick.

"I have my moments," Jared said, "but all kidding aside, this is some big shit, and the plan you laid out for me last night isn't the answer."

"I'm afraid to ask."

"This isn't about manning up and doing the right thing."

"I'm not running out on them," Reese said.

"I understand that, but expecting her to suck it up and move in with you isn't going to work, either. I take it that's why last night's conversation with her didn't end well."

"This isn't your business." Reese knew he was being rude, and worse, rude to his boss, in his boss' own home, but he had barely digested the situation himself. The last thing he needed was Jared up his jock.

Or maybe it was exactly what he needed.

"You made it my business," Jared said sternly. "Both you and Frank are like family, and I also have a station to run, and the last thing I need is a shit-ton of drama from the two of you."

"I don't mean to put you in an uncomfortable situation."

Jared arched one brow, while tilting his head to the side. "You're joking, right? I pick your ass up while you're babbling all sorts of crazy shit. You sleep on my couch, and all you got is 'you don't mean to put me in an uncomfortable situation'? That shit isn't going to fly anymore."

Reese nodded, knowing he'd have to be honest

with Jared about everything. Even if it meant opening up a vein full of old wounds.

"Answer me this," Jared said. "Do you, deep down, truly know you want the baby?"

Reese admired Jared's directness, but he didn't always know how to respond to it. It wasn't that he didn't want the baby. He'd vowed no child of his would be fatherless.

After Jessica, he disconnected his heart. He promised himself he'd never love again. He would never have children. He would live out his life without allowing that kind of pain. He hadn't known what a lonely existence that was until just now.

"It was unexpected," Reese said, "but yeah, I want the baby. Very much so." He wanted Patty. But one thing at a time.

"Wait for me outside."

"Why?" Reese asked.

"Just do it. Ryan," Jared yelled. "Reese and I are heading out for a while."

Reese waited out by the Jared's SUV while Jared kissed his wife and children goodbye. Ryan was a good ten years younger than Jared. Reese had heard some stories about them, but ultimately, they were the 'it' couple. The couple that beat the odds. The couple by which all other couples were measured.

Reese suddenly felt very small. Insignificant in the scheme of things. Being in a child's life, and being its father, were two entirely different things.

And he had never experienced either one.

"Where are we going?" Reese asked.

"Just follow me."

Reese got in his beat-up old Ford and did as instructed. At first, he thought they were headed to the station, but Jared made a turn off the main road, and then a few more, into an unfamiliar section just north of the village.

Jared pulled into a cemetery. Reese got out of his truck, then followed him down a winding path, covered in melting snow, to a tombstone. Both men remained silent.

Reese read the words on the tombstone: *Johnny Blake*.

"My son," Jared said.

Reese felt his heart slow as he held his breath for a long moment. A slow chill crept up his spine. He couldn't even imagine what might have happened. "I'm sorry. I didn't know you and Ryan had another child." Living with that kind of loss every day had to be impossible, yet Jared was the strongest, kindest man Reese had ever met. There were no words, but he said once again, "I'm sorry."

"Johnny was with my first wife. He died when he was six months old."

A long silence filled the warming air. Reese didn't know what to say, or if he should say anything at all, so he stood there with his hands in pockets and waited while Jared knelt and ran his fingers across the letters that spelled out his son's name.

"I got married because Lisa was pregnant. It was an awful marriage, and Johnny wasn't enough for us to even come close to making it work. She skipped out on us before Johnny died."

"I'm sorry for your loss," Reese said, humbled by the tremor in Jared's voice.

"I don't know what is really going on with you right now, and I'm not going to ask you to tell me unless you want to. But I do know"—Jared rose and pointed to his son's grave—"that whatever it was, it's as devastating to you as it was for me to lose my son."

"I don't think my situation is—"

"My son's death ruled my life for years. It prevented me from seeing what had always been right in front of me. It almost stopped me from allowing myself to fall in love with Ryan, and more importantly, to let her in and accept her love back."

"I appreciate all you're doing, but—"

Jared cut him off. "Whatever haunts you, deal with it and let it go, or you have no chance with Patty or your child. The baby needs to matter more. Lisa could never give that to Johnny."

Reese stared long and hard at the tombstone. His heart torn for the life lost and for the life he was about to bring into this world. His stomach knotted once again. He cared for Patty. But before he could really move forward with any kind of relationship with her, whatever that may be, he needed to deal with Jessica. With his past. Once and for all.

He understood that whatever came of him and Patty, he was going to be a father.

A real one. He was going to do whatever it took to be a good father, and hopefully win over the heart of the mother of his child.

They belonged together. Every fiber of his being believed that, but it would be hard to prove it to Patty.

Actions spoke louder than words.

They walked in silence back to the parking lot. The sun beat down on his face as the spring air rolled across the mountains like a kite took to the wind. The moment his mother had told him Allen wasn't his father, that he was in prison, and she wasn't going to tell him who his real father had been, a part of him had disappeared. His real father, whoever he was, hadn't been given the choice to decide for himself if he wanted a relationship.

The rest of him died when Jessica aborted their baby.

At least Patty was giving him the choice.

And the chance.

Driving back up Route 9, Reese noticed, behind a melting pile of snow, that The Heritage Inn was for sale. He remembered staying there and the old man that ran the place. It was quaint. Needed some work. But a nice family place.

Maybe a nice place to start. Maybe he should buy it.

He laughed at himself, but he realized he was dead serious. He'd worked as a bellhop for three summers in high school. Owning a hotel would be very different, but doable, and with a child on the way, and considering the most recent events with Patty, maybe being a cop and in the line of fire wasn't such a good career choice for a father.

Reese checked the time as he did a quick U-turn toward the store.

Might as well start over right now.

Patty was in her kitchen making some tea when she saw Reese's truck pull in. She wasn't expecting him, yet she had wanted to talk to him all day but figured they both needed a little time to process everything, and anyway, he would be working. He often took weekend shifts and extra shifts so family men could be home with their wives and children.

Reese was a good man. No denying that.

She had deep feelings for him. No denying that, either.

But Reese held back. Even Frank, who was probably Reese's closest friend in Lake George, said he held back from the whole male bonding thing.

That spoke volumes on all things regarding human relationships.

Did Reese really want a child, and would he be able to bond with it? She might not know the answers to those questions until after the baby was born.

That was a long time to be uncertain about anything, especially something as important as this, but she had to give him the opportunity without trapping him. That, she felt, was the key to her future, and to her child's happiness.

Her doorbell rang, pulling her from her deep thoughts.

"Sorry to stop by unannounced," Reese said. "I saw your car and I wanted to stop by and give you this." He held up a colorful bag with tissues coming out of the top, obviously a gift. "May I come in?"

"Sure." She took the gift, noticing her hand shook a little. She told herself she was still dealing with the trauma of the shooting, which was true, but the current tremor was all about the man who had just brought her a present and was now making himself comfortable on her sofa. "Would you like a drink?"

"I'll take a beer if you have one."

"I have some from the last...." Her cheeks heated, remembering one particular evening, one that most likely resulted in the conception of their child. She placed the beer on a coaster, next to the gift. "What's that for?"

"For you," he said. "Well, not really for you, it's for... Just open it."

She sat on the other side of the sofa, as far away from Reese as possible. She pulled out the tissue paper, then a couple of different generic baby outfits, bibs, pacifiers, and a Winnie the Pooh baby book.

Reese took the book in his hands, shifting closer to her. "This was my all-time favorite book when I was a little boy."

"Thank you," she said, folding up the tiny clothes; a mix of excitement and trepidation tingled through her fingers as she felt the cotton. The clothes were so tiny, and a surge of love hit her so hard she could barely breathe. "I'm really having a baby."

"You sound as shocked as I feel."

"I kind of am," she admitted. "I took the pregnancy test five times before I believed it, and even then, I went to the doctor and asked for a blood test." She scooted to the back of the couch, stuffing a pillow behind her back, sitting cross-legged, facing Reese and the lake. "You have to believe I didn't plan this."

"I know." Reese nodded. "I redacted my transfer."

"I don't want you to do that just because of the baby." *Or me,* she thought, though she knew he'd never stick around just for her.

"I am doing it because of the baby," he said. "And there is nothing wrong with that. But I also think we need to start over. With us."

"What do you mean?"

"Dating," he said, his face serious, but his eyes gave away his playfulness. Was that attraction and desire in his eyes, or was it something else? She had no idea, but no matter what, she couldn't allow herself to go in too deep with him. Not now. And maybe never.

"We've done that," she said.

"Not really. We had set up these ground rules, making it clear things wouldn't, couldn't go anywhere and I don't want that. I want us to start over. Do it right."

"There is a right way to date?" She stifled her laugh. Dating wasn't the answer. Being together wasn't the answer.

"I'm serious. I think it's best for the baby if his or her parents at least give it a go. Really see if there is something more between us."

Patty shook her head. "I don't want to get into a fight, and that is where this conversation is going. You know how I feel about my childhood. I don't want that for my child."

Reese closed the gap between them, placing his hands on her knees. She wanted to tear her gaze from him, but she couldn't. As he positioned himself to move in for a kiss, her lips parted, and he took that as invitation. He brushed his full luscious lips gently against hers. They were soft and tender and filled with the promise of what could be. Of what she wanted it to be. Of what she knew it couldn't be.

She grabbed a wad of his shirt, then pushed him away.

"You like me," he said, smiling at her with a twinkle in his eyes that she'd never seen before. It was playful and sweet. Kind and caring and at the same time pure raw passion.

All aimed at her.

"I never said I didn't, but liking each other and being a couple with a baby does not make a relationship." God, she sounded so cold.

"We've got to start somewhere." His breath was hot on her flesh. "I want to kiss you again, but only if you want me to."

For the life of her, she couldn't push him away. She found herself wrapping her arms around his neck, easing his body closer as he lowered himself onto her, pressing her back against the couch. And then he stopped abruptly, helping her to a sitting position again. "Wow," he managed. "We take this slowly. We date. That's all for now."

"You're the one who started that," she said, blushing with the knowledge that she would have jumped right in the sack with him.

"I just needed to know."

"Know what?"

"That you at least feel something for me. That we feel something for each other."

"Sexual attraction does not make a relationship."

"Please stop doing that," he said. "Your mouth is telling me to go away, but every other part of you says you want to give this a go as much as I do."

"I'm so confused by everything," she said. "We're giving each other mixed signals. You want to spend time with me. I like that. I want to spend time with you, but then you kiss me and we go right back to what got us into this situation in the first place. But your past. All this talk of living together and the baby, it makes me pull back."

"For now, we take things slow," he said. His tone gave away his hurt feelings. She didn't blame him for that. She felt it too. So much of their relationship had been about not being in a relationship that now that they wanted to give it a go, it was awkward. "Maybe we can get a bite to eat tonight."

"I've got dinner plans with some friends," she said. "So, if you will excuse me..."

"Sure. Another time." He took her hand and kissed it. "I'll see myself out."

She didn't get off the couch, nor did she let her breath out until after he closed the door.

This was not what she had expected from Reese.

Not at all. And it was messing with her well-laid-out plan for raising this baby alone. She had never handled things well when her plans were interrupted or altered.

While the baby and Reese were not an interruption, they were certainly causing a conflict that sent her senses in a tailspin.

Chapter Three

Reese sat at his designated desk in the middle of the big room in the trooper station, waiting for his new partner while searching the internet for his current wife. Why had he left without a getting a divorce? It seemed stupid now, but at the time, he couldn't stand to look at Jessica, much less talk to her, so he'd disappeared back into the ranks of the Marines, and she never tried to contact him once.

Now that he had a baby on the way, and things were looking up with Patty, it was time to bite the bullet and face the soon-to-be-ex-wife firing squad.

The station house wasn't very big, a satellite office for Troop G of the New York State Police. The big room contained six desks, crammed in the middle. Large florescent lights glared from the ceiling, bouncing off the scuffed, dull white floor. There was a small lobby with one metal desk. Off to the lobby's left stood one tiny office for Jared's secretary. Jared's office was in the back.

The station consisted of two support staff and eight to twelve troopers depending on the time of year, with more during the summer to manage activity on the lake. Jared had been the headman in this office nearly eight years now. Frank, Reese, Stacey, and five other troopers were assigned full-time duty to the area.

"I heard you had quite the time of it a couple of nights ago," Stacey said as she tossed her oversized parka on the coat rack by the front door. It was approaching forty-five degrees outside. Not parka weather by any means.

"That coat isn't standard issue."

"I'm in uniform." She smiled at him. "And I do have the proper coat, but that sucker doesn't really keep one warm, now does it?"

"It's nearly shorts weather."

She ignored the jab. She was the youngest trooper in the office, and when he first met her, he'd wondered if she was even legal to drink. He soon found out not only was she of age, she'd graduated with a degree in Criminal Psychology, and then graduated top of her class at the academy. She had blond hair, tucked up in a bun at the nape of her neck, and soft-brown eyes with an edge to them that said she was one tough nut.

"So, want to talk about it?" Stacey asked.

"Nothing to talk about."

"Not what my dad and his partner say."

Reese motioned to the desk across from his. "Do I want to know what they say?"

She put her Stetson on the desk, then took a seat. She sat up tall, folded her hands on the desk, and continued to stare at Reese with unnerving concentration. "A drunk cop who decided to take on my dad in a game of pool and lost his shirt."

"Wonderful."

"My father wanted to take you home. So did Doug. They do shit like that kind of often."

"Who is Doug?" He opted not to comment on what they might do often.

"His partner."

"Your dad's gay?" Normally, Reese wouldn't mess around like this with someone he didn't know well, but in the last two weeks, he found Stacey had almost no filter and a better sense of humor than anyone in this office, even if she was a bit on the young side. Besides, it was a legit question when you referred to two men as partners without any qualifiers.

She rolled her eyes. "Business partner," she said. "They were going to bring you home, but Mary, Doug's wife, had a fit. They're staying at my dad's place for a few days while my dad and Doug put in her new cabinets."

"And why weren't you out and about the other night?" Reese asked. "Oh wait, you're not old enough to drink yet."

Her brow tightened. "I'll be twenty-two next month, thank you very much."

Considering everything he knew about her, she could have gone on to a top-level government job at the CIA, FBI, or any other Alphabet agency, and made a shitload of money. And it would probably be a bit more exciting.

"Besides," she continued, the words coming as fast as the credits at the end of a movie, "I can't stand Doug's wife, and the feeling is mutual, and Doug and my dad don't like my boyfriend, and he's here visiting, and we wanted some time alone, so there is that."

"Anyone ever tell you that you offer too much information?"

"Anyone ever tell you that you don't offer enough?"

"Point taken," he said. "Why be a trooper? You could have done anything with your degree."

"Because I like it here."

"You might not be stationed here forever, you know."

"I am for now."

"Where's your boyfriend? You mentioned he was visiting."

Jared stepped out of his office. "Stacey Sutten, you file those reports?"

"Yes, sir."

"Stacey," Jared said. "Stop with the 'sir' crap. I've known you since you were in diapers."

"I just won twenty bucks," Stacey said, pumping the air with her fist. Her smile was wider than the one on a kid in a candy shop.

"No, you didn't," Jared said. "Your dad said that bet was if I said I changed your diaper, and that, my dear child, I will never cop to."

"But you did change my diapers."

Jared just shook his head and went back into his office.

"Do you have any idea how weird that conversation was?" Reese asked.

"That's normal for us." Stacey leaned back in her chair and crossed her legs. She was an attractive young woman, but she put out a "keep away from me because I bite" vibe. Her dry sense of humor seemed to be a personality trait, but Reese recognized it was also a defense mechanism.

"Got to be weird, being a trooper in the town you grew up in."

"Haven't been a trooper that long, so I don't know. But it will be fun to pull over some of the assholes I had to deal with in high school."

"Yeah, I could see how that would be fun," he said. "How does your dad feel about you being a cop?"

"He hates it, but I wasn't about to become a partner in the Sutten & Tanner Construction Company—not because I'm not qualified, but because my dad doesn't think it's ladylike."

"And being a cop is?"

She tilted her head and gave a ladylike smile. "My father once told me I couldn't handle construction, after he told me it was man's work. He's so old-fashioned it's insane, and it's not like he's that old. He let me work with him and Doug for a summer. He told me I needed to go out in the world and carve my own way before he'd consider hiring me. I went off to college, studied criminal law, and decided to be a cop. My dad nearly passed out when I told him, then he offered me a job."

Three times, Reese tried to interject to tell her to slow down or take a breath, or just shut up, but he didn't see the point. It was fun to listen to her ramble anyway.

"I think I've met your dad's partner over at Harmon Hill," Reese said. "Oh, and I met the Nesbitch, too. At least that's what Frank called her."

Stacey roared with laughter. "No one likes Doug's wife. Not sure how much Doug likes her. They got married because she was pregnant, but then she lost the baby. Doug really wants kids, and she says she does, but she's too busy with her career. I give them six more months, tops."

His heart skipped a beat as he visualized Patty being held at gunpoint. When it had happened, he had no idea she carried his baby. The idea something could have happened to Patty, or his baby, made his stomach churn. "You really need to learn to filter what you say." She had no way of knowing his personal situation with Patty or his hopefully soon-to-be ex-wife, but still, Stacey was going to need to mature and learn sometimes less was more.

She rolled her eyes again. "I'm not saying

anything that isn't out there in the universe for all to know, or something I wouldn't say to their faces."

"Maybe Doug and his wife don't want their laundry discussed over and over again."

"Now you sound like my father."

"Your father is a smart man." Reese decided it was time to redirect the conversation and take advantage of this walking font of gossip. "What do you know about The Heritage Inn?"

"My dad would love to get his hands on The Heritage Inn. He and Doug have too much equity tied up in other projects right now and can't buy it, but if they had the funds, they would."

"What would they do with it?"

"Restore it, and then find a buyer so some big land developer doesn't come in and rip the place down. The woodwork inside the main hotel is exquisite. You should see the staircase. And the cottages? So adorable. There is also a house on the property, where the original owners—"

"You're going to hyperventilate," Reese said. "Can you just answer my questions with a simple response?"

She crossed her arms and gave him the best smart-ass smile she could muster. "Sure."

"What does a place like that go for?"

"Millions," she said. "That direct enough for you?" Her smile was as playful as the sarcasm dripping in her words. He was going to like working with her, babbling mouth and all.

"If you know so much about this, why not take your dad up on his offer and take over the family business?"

"Because my dad would put me in an office and give me some stupid title that would prevent me from getting my hands dirty. When I was little, he kept trying to make me into a prissy little girl, and this was my way of rebelling."

"Being top of your class at the academy is an interesting way to rebel."

"Should have seen what I did at some beauty pageant my father put me in when I was ten. He was mortified, but I think he realized I wasn't a prissy little girl," she said. "But getting back to your problem, buying something like The Heritage Inn. You should file a plan when you place the offer. With a bid like that, it's best if you have a plan, and best if that plan feeds into what is already there, and how any changes you make will enhance the area."

This young lady was turning out to be one surprise after the other. "Who says I want to buy, much less have the money?"

"I don't know about the money, but I can tell by the sound of your voice and the look in your eye you want to buy. You know, my dad might help finance something like that, especially if you're going to keep it basically as it is."

"You really think your dad might be able to help?" He didn't need the financing, but he would certainly hire the man.

"If you're serious, I'll give him a call later to see what he says."

"I'm serious." He snagged his iPhone, pulling up Patty's contact information. But what would he text? That he found them the perfect home? A place where they would be happy. Where their child could have everything he or she ever needed or wanted. A place where they could grow old together. A place where it would be okay, no matter what?

He couldn't say that, so he opted for 'let's have a date night; we need to talk.' It was better than nothing.

Patty dreaded going into work. It had only been two days out from the shooting. She should have told Conrad to piss off, but he'd always been good to her.

She had full benefits, and he paid her well, treated her well, and the shooting wasn't his fault. None of that reasoning made her feel any better. Nor did it stop the slight tremor she had in her hands. Too much had been at stake during those few hours when a stranger threatened her life and the very existence of her unborn child. She questioned her sanity as she pulled into the office parking lot.

She entered the building, surprised the window to her office had already been fixed. The receptionist, Angela, was on the phone, but greeted her with a nod and smile as she handed Patty a stack full of folders, a few phone messages, and note from Conrad. "Can you hold please?" Angela asked, then set down the phone. She was in her mid-sixties and had worked for Conrad for the last eight months. She had snow-white hair. "I can't believe he's making any of us come in."

"The world hasn't stopped for everyone," Patty said, though she knew the words fell flat as she hugged the receptionist. "Sometimes it's best if we all move on with life." She wanted to believe the words she had spoken, but what she really wanted was to spend a few days in bed, alone, watching mindless television.

"I've got to get back to this call." Angela gave

Patty a good squeeze. "Conrad wants you in the conference room." Had it not been for Angela, Patty might not be alive.

Patty walked down the hall, hesitating at the spot where Matt had been shot in her doorway. A floor mat currently covered the stains. The hair on the back of her neck stood upright, and she shuddered at the memory. Matt would be fine, though he was still in the hospital after having extensive surgery, but would either of them ever recover emotionally?

Her office had been cleaned, and Conrad had managed to put in a new wood desk and a nice new office chair. What little blood had trickled from her wound had been successfully removed from the carpet. She placed both hands over her belly, thinking about how precious life, or the potential of life, was.

The stacks of paper on the new desk had been straightened, and someone had placed a large bouquet of flowers on the corner. The arrangement was filled with tulips, a sure sign of summer. She smiled. The only reason she knew the flowers were tulips was because Reese was so into gardening it was weird. The card read *Welcome back—Conrad.*

She dumped her new workload on the desk, took off her coat, and then headed toward the conference room with a bottle of water in one hand, and a pencil and legal pad in the other.

The conference room was an oval room with glass all around it. As she rounded the corner toward it past Conrad's office, she noticed the two office associates, Ben and Russ, at the end with Conrad, and across the table sat four unfamiliar men. Conrad waved her in.

"Everyone, this is our other paralegal, Patty Harmon. She'll be doing most of the grunt work on this. Patty, this is Mister Keith Holland of Holland Development. You may have seen him around before...the unfortunate incident."

"Nice to meet you," Patty said, doing her best to push 'the unfortunate incident' from her mind's eye.

"The pleasure is all mine," Keith said. "I'm so sorry about what my previous employee did to you."

"Previous employee?" Patty felt a wave a nausea as she made the connection to the man that had held her, and her baby, at gunpoint. She was also a bit surprised by the color of Keith's eyes, the same bright ice-blue as Reese's. Not a forgettable color.

"Terry worked for my company, though I'd never met him. He was stealing from me, and Conrad figured it out. I'm so glad you and your coworkers will be okay. If there is anything I can ever do for you, please, just ask."

"Thanks," she said, wishing this meeting would come to a quick end so she could go home. This was harder than she thought it would be.

"Patty," Conrad said, "can you pull up the deeds and do title searches for The Heritage Inn and Kendrick's Paper properties?"

"Not a problem."

"Also, can you work on filing a motion to get the financials on The Heritage Inn? Shouldn't be too hard, since it's for sale. The hotel closed at the end of the season, but I heard a couple of the cottages are still rented through the rest of the winter season, so find out who is managing that."

"The real-estate is handling that," Ben said. He always spoke more than Russ, though neither of them spoke often, but they were good lawyers. "Once those renters vacate, the hotel and the cottages will officially shut down."

"Anything else?" Patty asked.

"Yes," Conrad said. "Find out from the real-estate what other property listings are comparable to The Heritage Inn could be going on the market."

"I'm looking for something with a house, and perhaps a couple of guest houses or an inn. Bed-and-breakfast type places with a decent amount of land and water frontage."

"Any particular area? I know there are some on the east side of the lake, but much farther north." Patty scribbled a few notes on her legal pad, which she thought should make her feel normal. Comfortable in her workplace. But all it did was remind her of being held at gunpoint.

"I'd prefer to be closer to the village, if possible," Keith said. "Any chance of keeping this quiet? We really want to weigh our options."

She added it to her list. "The moment I do a title search, it's going to create some buzz."

"Then do that last," Keith said.

"All right," Patty said.

"Thank you." Keith motioned to the other men from his company. "Once the casino is up, I'm going to enjoy living here full time."

"Anything else I can do?" Patty hated the idea of someone like this man owning the property next to Harmon Hill. She couldn't put her finger on it, and assumed she was just affected by the shooting, but this man gave her the creeps.

"That's it for now," Holland said. "We'd best be on our way. We'll be in touch."

"Let me show you out," Patty said.

"I'll join you," Conrad added.

Ben and Russ were passing papers back and forth, talking quietly between themselves. They were related somehow to Conrad, though she wasn't sure how. Ben was just out of law school, so this was his first job, and Russ was about five years older. Both men kept to themselves, only communicating with Patty when absolutely necessary.

Keith stopped at the front door. "Again, I can't tell you how sorry I am for what happened. I wish there was something I could do to make it up to you."

"I appreciate it, but it's over with," Patty said. "I'd prefer just to put it behind me." She shook Keith's hand, then watched him and his entourage leave the building.

"I appreciate you coming in," Conrad said. "With our caseload, and Matt on medical leave, I need someone on this full time."

"Can I do some of this from home? I'm still a bit shaken up." She clasped her hands together, trying to keep them from shaking as she stood just ten feet from where Matt had been shot. "I'm uncomfortable being here right now."

"Of course you can," Conrad said. "Holland is a

big client. He brings in a lot of billing hours, and he's going to bring us more."

"I understand," she said. "I'll take all this home for now. I'll report in later."

"I'm good with that."

Patty gathered her belongings, along with four full boxes of paperwork, and made a beeline for her car. She couldn't get out of that office fast enough. So many unsavory memories flooded her mind she thought she might go crazy staying there another second. It was going to be a long night.

"I need to make a phone call." Reese signed his end-of-shift report while Stacey put the keys to the patrol car away in Jared's office. He had thought this assignment would be nothing but a pain in the ass, but Stacey was capable, smart, and damn funny. "Are you sure your dad won't mind us dropping in?"

"You're dropping in. I live there. No 'us' in the equation."

"I see." He laughed. "And now I remember how young you really are."

"My age has nothing to do with my living arrangements," she said. "Once my boyfriend finishes law school and moves here, I'll be moving in with him."

Reese figured that might be over her father's dead body. "And where is the boyfriend now?"

"Columbia University." She headed toward the door, wrapping herself in her large, non-issue parka.

It really isn't that cold out, Reese thought. "You're going to wait for me, right? I'll follow you."

"I'll be in my car," she said, "waiting for you, old man."

He shook his head, then punched in the speed dial for Patty on his phone. It went straight to voice-mail. "Can you meet me tonight? I'll text you with the details. Probably around nine, if that's okay."

He ended the call, and then dialed a number he never kept in any phone or address book, anywhere. He probably should, but it was nice to actually know someone's phone number without asking Siri for it.

Elizabeth answered on the first ring. "So, you got my email." Her voice indicated she was a little pissed and very disappointed.

"Well, hello to you, too, Nana." Reese called her sometimes twice a week, but it had been over ten days now, and while he had good enough excuses, they were still excuses.

"Hello, Reese," she said softly, but the edge

hadn't disappeared. "I don't hear diddly from you, then I get this email with a bunch of documentation for a bid on a hotel, saying you need it all signed, with bank statements, and you need it yesterday. Mind telling me what the heck is going on? I nearly got in the car and hauled ass north."

Reese had been so private with his personal life that Nana had never once visited him anywhere in the last seven years. He made it down to see her every three or four months. It had been nearly four months since their last visit.

"I think the documentation speaks for itself."

"Don't be coy and cute with me," she said. "Why do you want to buy a fallen-down hotel?"

"It's not fallen-down. Just needs a little TLC."

"Whatever," Nana said, full of her usual piss and vinegar. "Why do you want to buy it? And if you mention a woman, we're going to need to have a long talk."

"It's complicated."

"Everything with you and women has either been complicated or nonexistent." The disdain oozing with her words spoke volumes. "So, this purchase is because of a woman?" The suspicion and trepidation in her voice grew.

Reese wasn't sure how to answer that because he

hadn't sorted out the Patty situation, and he wasn't about to give his grandmother a heart attack over the phone by telling her about the baby. "It's complicated." Besides, he didn't want her to 'haul ass' north and give Patty the third degree.

"I don't like it when you say that. I'll need to have her vetted."

"So not necessary."

"I beg to differ," Nana said.

"We'll talk more when I come to visit, but I need access to a large sum of money, along with your signatures on the offer, now. If this goes through, maybe it's time you sell the house and move up here. Get away from the city."

"White Plains is not the city," she corrected. "Please tell me you're not buying this hotel for this woman. Or with this woman. Reese, you haven't always been—"

"That was one mistake, Nana, and I won't ever repeat it again," he said, though considering Patty was pregnant, Nana might see this as more of not learning from his mistakes. "This purchase is for me. For a future, and once I own the hotel, you could move here with me. Wouldn't you like that?"

His grandmother let out a long sigh. "You know I've been talking about selling this place. Making a change. I'm not getting any younger and I know you won't ever live here again."

"So, you're going to do this favor for me?"

"Normally, I'd say, 'Anything for my favorite grandson,' but right now, I'm very disappointed, therefore you are no longer the favorite."

"I'm your only grandson," Reese said, knowing her chiding hid a world of hurt and frustration. "I understand your concern, but my job is good, and I want to stay here. Permanently."

"I've heard that before."

"That was different," Reese said. "Can I get access to the money?"

"I've already set up an account that you can use to finalize the offer, if you get it. But no woman will be on the title other than me, got it?"

"Yes, ma'am," he said. "Now, I've got a crazy question for you."

"Crazier than you wanting money to buy a hotel?"

Well, here goes nothing, he thought. "Does Jessica's family still live in Jersey?"

"I haven't seen her or her family since that dreadful day. Why the hell do you want to know?"

"Because I never divorced her."

Total silence on the other end. "Nana?" Reese

checked his phone, noting a text from Stacey that she was going to leave his sorry old ass behind. The idea that he was actually getting older made him realize it was time. He was going to be a dad, something that he never thought he'd look forward to.

"I'm here, plotting ways to toss you over my knee and whip you with your grandfather's belt, may he rest in peace."

"If it's any consolation, I'm still technically broke, so she won't be getting any of your money if she tries to fight dirty," Reese said.

"I can't believe you think she'd be anything less than unfair and downright ruthless," she said. "But I'll see what I can find out about that little witch." The line went dead.

Reese was betting on two things: first, by putting down roots, he'd show Patty he wasn't the kind of man to ever hurt her or their child, and that he was in it for the long haul. How he was going to prove that was left to be seen.

Second, he loved her. Just admitting it to himself took a load off his shoulders. He couldn't just tell her, because she'd think he only said it out of obligation. Or that he felt trapped. He understood her reasoning behind those feelings. He'd never given her any reason to believe differently. But he was determined to start making his life uncomplicated in the female department. That meant he needed to prove to Patty that any action he took from this point forward wasn't because she was pregnant, but because he wanted what that pregnancy offered. Family.

A real family. That he was all in on. Now it was time to prove it.

Stacey was already in her vehicle, and her mouth was moving as fast as her hands; she was obviously on the phone and not happy. He waved. She waved back but continued talking on the Bluetooth device. The girl had a lot of spunk, but she talked way too much and way too fast. But that wasn't his problem. Right now, he needed to show Patty he meant business.

Actions, not words.

He followed Stacey back through the village, past Million Dollar Beach, and then up Assembly Point, all the while wondering how to buy The Heritage Inn. There was a lot to consider, but he'd make it work.

Stacey pulled into a driveway containing two big black pickup trucks with Sutten & Tanner Construction painted in bright white letters on the sides. The house was older, but huge, and it looked as if everything had been remodeled. A two-car detached garage stood on the far side of what could have been a mini parking lot, and the house also had a three-car attached garage.

"Wow," he said as he got out of the car. "I've seen this house from the lake. It's fantastic."

"My dad bought it when I was a baby and restored it. I guess it was in pretty bad shape, and he got it for next to nothing." She ran her hands over one of the trucks. "Looks like you get both my dad and his business partner tonight."

"That's a good thing, right?"

"Depends on how much you like to get harassed."

"Wonderful." He followed her down the pathway toward the main garage. The house was very private, sitting on the last lot on the point. The evening sky was clear and thankfully, the wind was nonexistent. It wasn't parka cold out, but he'd left his fleece behind.

"Before we go in, I need to warn you about something that you won't remember from your last encounter with my dad and his partner."

"I don't remember anything about it, anyway."

She laughed. "My dad is a little weird, and his partner even weirder, and since I didn't have the chance to tell them you were coming, it might be downright bizarre."

"So I really am just dropping in."

"I meant to firm up the details since I texted them earlier, but I got into a discussion with Todd on the ride home."

"Who's Todd?"

"My boyfriend."

"All right," Reese said, feeling awkward.

She opened the door, and he followed her through a small hallway into the kitchen, where a man sat at the table reading the paper and drinking a beer. A younger man with shoulder-length dark hair, wearing an apron, was cooking something over the stove. The cook seemed to be about the same age as Reese. The one at the table didn't appear to be old enough to be Stacey's father.

"Hey, baby girl," said the man at the table without looking up. "How was your day? Shoot anyone?"

"Har, har," she said.

He looked up then. "Well, who did you bring home?"

"Dad—"

"You're the drunk dude from the other night,"

the long-haired guy said. "You still owe me twenty bucks."

"Since I don't remember betting you, I'm going to wager that I don't have to pay that bet." Reese shook the younger man's hand. "Sorry if I offended anyone."

Both men laughed. "You were highly entertaining," Stacey's father said. "Does this mean Todd is chopped liver? I'll take this drunk over Stupid Face any day of the week."

"Oh, my God, Dad. Really. This is my partner, boss, and trainer, Reese." She kissed her father on the cheek. "Reese, this is my dad, Jim, and that guy over there with the spatula is his work wife, Doug."

Spatula Guy waved. "For the most part, ignore Jim, except when it comes to Todd. He really is a weasel, and we'd both love to see her dump him."

"Drop it." Stacey waved her finger at Doug. "It's not like my dad likes your choice in women any better."

Doug shook his head. "I'm not his daughter. There is a difference."

"Where is the little woman?" Stacey chided. "Working late? Out of town? What you think of Todd is exactly what I think of her."

"You need to be more concerned about how disrespectful the weasel is toward your dad."

Reese didn't know the man, but Doug's tone was neither playful nor upbeat. Stacey's was even worse.

"Play nice, children," Jim said, "and get our guest a beer."

Reese felt like he'd just entered a Twilight Zone with a state-of-the-art kitchen. Richly stained hardwood floors. Granite counters. The cabinets matched the floors, and all the appliances were top-of-the-line stainless steel. A large oak table stood in the middle of the huge space.

"A beer would be great," Reese said.

Jim folded his paper, then put it on the table. "Have a seat. So, you're not after my daughter's honor, which is too bad, really, because we'd help pave the way."

"I'm just looking into the possible purchase and renovation of The Heritage Inn, sir."

"Dad," Stacey said sternly. "Would you mind not trying to sell me off to my boss?"

"Jared is your boss. This guy is—"

"This isn't funny," Stacey muttered.

Jim nodded. "Sorry. So what can we do for you, Reese?"

Doug put a plate in front of Jim and one in front of Reese.

Reese looked down at the plate, which contained toast with some beef and white sauce. "Thanks. I haven't had shit on a shingle in years."

"It's the only thing Doug can cook," Stacey said.

"Well, at least I can cook something healthy. All you can do is bake cookies."

"I could shoot you between the eyes from a mile away," Stacey said. "And I'd look damn good doing it, too."

"Both of you shut up. You're worse than toddlers fighting over a pacifier," Jim said.

Reese laughed.

Stacey and Doug shot Jim daggers. Jim smiled widely. Interesting family. Explained a lot about Stacey.

"Thanks for dinner," Reese said. He hadn't realized he was hungry, but he dug in. Doug sat on his left, and Stacey on his right. It was actually kind of nice. Sort of like being at the Harmons', except with fewer people and double the sarcasm.

"Reese is interested in the Heritage property," Stacey said between bites.

"Really?" Jim raised his brow.

"Wish we could have bought that place," Doug

said. "Heard just today that there is some interest by an outsider. Just hope they want to restore it, not destroy it."

"I'm thinking about buying the place," Reese said, surprised he had possible competition.

"What are your plans, son?" Jim asked, his tone serious.

"I want to restore it, modernize it a bit, and make it one of the go-to family places on the south end of the lake. I want to put in an offer, but I admit I'm out of my element."

Doug and Jim exchanged a few looks, then nodded at each other.

"What do you mean by 'restore' and 'modernize'?" Doug asked.

"I mean to keep the structure, but make it more modern, more appealing to people wanting to stay a week or more. Add to the waterfront. Keep it a family place. There is a whole section of land that could be used to put in family-friendly activities like shuffle-boards, a basketball court, that sort of thing. I see it as more of a long-term cabin rental and small hotel."

Jim and Doug nodded at each other again.

Reese enjoyed their secret communication, but wished he was in on it. The Harmons did that kind of stuff all the time, and it drove him nuts. Hell, even Frank and Jared often had some kind of secret mind-reading going on.

"Why don't we take this discussion to the family room? Baby girl, how about some cookies?"

"Really, Dad? You want me to make cookies from scratch? Now?"

"I know you have frozen cookie dough hidden in the freezer."

"And how often have you dipped into that?" she asked, then started rummaging around the kitchen.

"I just make a couple every day to munch on at the site," Jim said. "Come on, Reese, let's go to the family room. Doug, any chance you have those blueprints?"

"I have some workups on my laptop. I'll go get it."

Reese followed Jim into the family room. It soared up the full two stories of the house, with a spiral staircase to one side, which led to a balcony and windows that overlooked the lake. Living in anything other than an apartment hadn't crossed Reese's mind in years. He didn't need much, so a small space suited him. A family, however, needs more than just a place to rest one's head. A family needed a place to gather and feel safe, and Reese wanted to provide that for his...family.

The family room opened to another room, probably the living room, and he saw a deck off that room. Next to the staircase, he saw a couple of doors, and on the other side of the room, a set of French doors. The house was huge, even compared to what he'd seen from the waterfront.

Reese didn't know what to say, so he said nothing. Instead, he sipped his beer and planted his butt on the sofa across from Jim's chair. They sat in silence for a few moments.

"How long have you lived here?" Jim asked.

"A couple of years. You?"

"My entire life. My folks live over on Cleverdale, about five houses down from Jared Blake. Your boss. Good man."

"He is," Reese said.

Doug walked in with a laptop already fired up, then placed it on the coffee table. "We have a few different blueprints of The Heritage Inn. A few we had done for the original owner a couple of years ago, and some we were considering if we could have bought the place ourselves."

Doug tapped the keyboard a few times, and a 3D image appeared. He clicked a few more keys, and the images rotated. "The cabins are all in good shape, so not much to do there, but here"—he pointed to the screen—"we thought of adding a few more cabins, a playground, tennis courts, and a few other family-friendly activities, as you mentioned." The images on the screen changed, showing the suggested layout. Doug tapped away again. "The main building has some problems, but if you gut the lobby, reconfiguring it like this"—he pointed to the screen as the plans replaced the old Heritage images—"you'll be able to get into all the walls and fix every problem, maybe breaking only half the bank. Everything else just needs to be updated, refinished, et cetera."

Reese took a long sip of his beer. Money wasn't the object. Winning over Patty was. "What about the main residence?"

"Nothing wrong with the house. It was built in the early seventies but renovated about ten years ago. I did the work on that. Would you plan on living there?"

"I guess so," Reese said. "Let me ask you this." He put his beer on the table and leaned forward, resting his elbows on his knees. "In its current condition, do you think the property is worth six-point-five million?"

"Yes," Jim and Doug answered at the same time.

"So what do you suggest I offer?"

Jim and Doug exchanged glances. "Not far under the asking price. Maybe six-point-two million," Jim said, "and I'd do it as soon as possible. Personal question, but do you have the money to offer top dollar?" Jim asked.

"I do," Reese admitted.

"And do all the necessary work?" Jim asked.

"I do," Reese said.

Stacey entered the family room, carrying a tray of freshly baked cookies. "What did I miss?" She'd changed from her uniform into jeans and a trooper sweatshirt. She'd also pulled her hair out of the bun, and it hung in waves to her waist.

"Reese is going to buy the Heritage," Jim said.

"I'm considering hiring your dad to do the work," Reese said.

"We can get you a list of references. Anything built on Harmon Hill in the last eight years, we've done both the construction and the design," Doug said. "Also, we're totally redesigning the Village Place. You can stop by anytime."

Reese didn't know a lot about construction or design, but he could tell quality work when he saw it, and Frank and Lacy had hired Sutten & Tanner to build their house. Add the fact they were locals that sealed the deal. "I think I'd like to retain your services now."

"We appreciate that," Jim said, "but feel free to look around. We won't take it personally."

"We can also sell you my designs," Doug said. "If you decide to go with someone else."

"I've seen your work on Harmon Hill, and I've heard from others that locally, you are the best in the business."

"If you really want to hire us, then you should include these plans in the offer," Doug said as he snagged a couple of cookies. "I'll get you copies, but we can make it all contingent on the sale."

"I'm meeting the real-estate agent tonight."

"We'll get you these plans by morning. Let the real-estate agent know that," Jim said.

Reese took a cookie, then nibbled on it while he considered what his nana would say about hasty decisions, but if someone else was interested in that land, he knew he should move quick. "Do I get the friends and family discount?"

"Yes," Jim said. "That said, it's going to take me a day or so to prepare an estimate."

"I appreciate that," Reese said. He finished his cookie, which he had to admit was the best damn cookie he'd ever had. "Do you need a deposit?"

"If we are filing the plans for you in the morning, that will cost five hundred, so if you can give that to us now, while we prepare a contract, we'd appreciate it. The final estimate will include a two-year, three-phase working plan that puts The Heritage Inn as a full rental facility starting next spring. Maybe even earlier. That's based on the work we've already put into it on our own."

"I'm looking forward to working with you," Reese said.

"We've wanted to work on that place for years," Jim said. "It's going to be a pleasure."

Reese enjoyed another cookie. All in all, it been an interesting and productive evening. Now he just had to tell Patty.

Chapter Four

atty waited nervously in the front seat of her car in the parking lot of The Heritage Inn. Being Reese's casual fling had been easy, but the idea of dating him seemed more bizarre than the fact that she was pregnant with his child. Meeting at The Heritage Inn? That was just weird. The property had been abandoned when the owners could no longer take care of it themselves. Last Patty heard, they'd been placed in assisted living. A run-down property seemed like a very odd place to meet indeed. She thought about suggesting the little café with the great chocolate cake, but curiosity got the better of her. She was seeing a new side to Reese. It was both delightful and terrifying.

Memories of her childhood made her heart flutter. As girls, she and LuAnn Riley, daughter of the owners of the inn, were inseparable. A fair amount of private land, owned by the Harmons, separated her from The Heritage Inn, but she could still walk through the lush trees to the Heritage family home, as she had so often done. At one point, the girls had made a path lined with reflectors. Once, they'd even pitched a tent in a small clearing and spent the night, until a group of raccoons scared them away. Later, they found that Frank and his friends had put food around the tent to draw them. She and LuAnn plotted for months on how to get the boys back, but they were nowhere near as devious.

Headlights flickered in her rearview mirror. Reese with someone she didn't recognize following behind him. She shut off the engine, then stepped from her car. Reese greeted her with a huge grin on his face and a playful twinkle in his eyes. It was a look she hadn't seen often on him, if ever. He looked light, carefree. Happy.

"Hey, there," he said. "I've got a surprise for you." He kissed her cheek.

She tilted her head so his lips landed in just the right place. They lingered on her skin, sending tingles to the rest of her body. "What are we doing here?" she asked, trying desperately to keep her cool.

This was all about becoming friends so they could co-parent. That was it. Nothing more. Nothing less.

The stranger he'd brought with him got out of his car and waved. He was older, most likely in his late fifties, wearing blue pants and a North Face coat. She recognized him then, from realty signs plastered all over town. Charlie Vicor, of Vicor Commercial Reality.

"Charlie, I'd like you to meet Patty Harmon."

"I've met your father a few times," Charlie said. "He's a good man."

"Yes, he is," Patty agreed. Drunk and depressed, but pretty good at putting on a show for the people outside the family until about a year ago.

"Let me show you around," Charlie said.

"Why are we looking at this place with a real-estate agent?" she whispered to Reese.

"Humor me." Reese took her by the arm, and they followed Charlie into the main lobby of The Heritage Inn. The furniture and wallpaper were dated, and it smelled a bit musty, but the view of the lake was breathtaking, just as she remembered.

"I was devastated when the Riley's closed the place," Charlie said. "My children loved to stay here when they came to visit, but neither of the Riley children wanted to take it over, and it was just too much for Harold. Then his wife got sick. What a shame. Sweet lady."

"I was close to LuAnn once," Patty said. "I lost touch with her after high school."

"She's some big designer in New York City," Charlie said proudly. "She's paying for her parents' living arrangements now. She really wanted to keep the property, but it just wasn't in the cards."

"Could we see the residential living quarters?" Reese asked.

Nostalgia overwhelmed Patty as she pictured herself as a small child racing between The Heritage Inn property with LuAnn, giggling without a care in the world

"Sure thing," Charlie said.

Reese's hand rested on her elbow, his thumb caressing ever so slightly, a gesture that could be seen as love, or simply a man who understood and respected other human beings.

Reese was the latter, never the former.

"LuAnn and I spent a lot of time on this front patio. Not to mention jumping off the huge sundeck over the boathouse as boats passed by." Patty left out that both girls had their first kiss on top of that boathouse.

The house sat on the north side of the property,

tucked up tight to the trees lining Harmon Hill. It had a separate driveway on the other side of the inn. The hotel and house stood next to each other, with only some overgrown trees and the driveway to separate them. A long path wound from the hotel to the house. The front lawn was massive, looping along a large stretch of the lakeshore. To the south side, the cottages sat closer to the water, with a small grassy parking area in back, and lots of land between them and Route 9. All the property needed was a little TLC and maybe some upgrades to attract more seasonal renters. They really were the bread and butter of the village, not the people who lived here year-round.

Charlie flicked on the back porch light, and they entered through the kitchen. It was as big as she remembered, furnished with new appliances, but the big butcher-block kitchen table was as exactly as she remembered.

"Six bedrooms," Charlie said. "Three stories, at a total of four thousand square feet."

"This is what we talked about." Reese handed Charlie an envelope. "They have until tomorrow at five to counter. The construction company will be filing the plans in the morning. I'm sure we can come to an agreement."

What agreement, Patty thought, but didn't ask because she was too busy remembering her favorite Barbie doll and how she and LuAnn would talk about what it would be like to be grown up, married, with a family...

"Excellent. Which company, so I can make sure everything is in order?"

"Sutten & Tanner."

"Excellent choice," Charlie said.

"Now, do you mind if we check the place out alone?"

Charlie nodded. "I'll be waiting in the car. Take your time."

Patty was so caught up in remembering that she ignored the two men talking, though she made a mental note to ask Reese about Sutten & Tanner. "LuAnn and I used to sit under this table with our Barbie dolls on rainy days when we were in grade school." Patty lost herself in the moment, gliding her fingers across the uneven wood. "When my parents would fight, I came here. LuAnn and her parents were like a second family to me."

"So, you have fond memories of this place?"

"Oh, yes," Patty said. "Why did you bring me here?"

"I just put in an offer."

"Huh...what? Offer? As in buy?" Her heart beat so fast it hurt. Reese's conversation with the real-estate agent pulled together. "You want to buy a hotel?"

"I do."

"How? The asking price on this place is like, what, over six million? How on earth can you afford that on your current salary? How can you run a hotel and be a trooper?"

"Let's just say we need to talk. About a lot of things."

"I have no idea what to say." Her mind raced with a million questions, but she couldn't bring a single one to her mouth. She blinked a few times, wondering if she was having a bizarre dream, because no way was Reese McGinn planning on buying a hotel. "I think I need to sit down."

"Why don't we just go back to your place? You can sit down, put your feet up. You're still limping. And we can talk about this and my plans to buy the hotel."

She pulled her coat tight around her middle and adjusted her purse strap. "This is all so sudden. I can't... I can't even process the idea that you would...could buy this place." The very idea that

Reese would buy a house was unnerving. This was over the top.

"I know it's sudden, but it feels so right," he said.

She wanted to trust his intentions. His big schoolboy grin. The excitement laced in his voice. His blue eyes danced with something she couldn't quite put her finger on, and it made her want to leap into his arms. Instead, she held on to what she didn't know about Reese and the fact he could rip her heart into tiny little pieces. "I've got a lot of questions." But first, she'd have to sort them all out in her head. "I expect honest answers. You can't dodge a single one or redirect me, like you always did when I asked you about your family, the military, where you lived..."

"I can do that," he said. "You good to drive? You look a little...a little—"

"I'm okay," she said. "I'll see you at my place in a few."

Patty drove the half mile up the hill from the parking lot of The Heritage Inn, then right on Route 9, and another half mile to the turn on Harmon Hill. All the while, Reese followed close behind. Reality started to sink in: he was going to stick around. She was just getting used to the idea that maybe they could nail this co-parenting thing. She held her breath on any thought of a relationship, unsure that the Reese she knew was capable of a totally honest, fully committed relationship.

How could she process this new Reese?

The cool evening air hit her face as she opened her car door. It had dropped to below freezing, and the weatherman was calling for flurries. She let Reese take her hand as they walked in silence up to her apartment. "Are you hungry?"

"I could eat something," he said. "Why don't I open a bottle of wine and get some cheese and crackers? You do have cheese and crackers?"

"I do," she said, "but no wine for me."

"Oh, yeah. Pregnant women probably shouldn't drink. So, what do you want instead?"

"There is some sparkling water in the fridge. I'll take a bottle of that. Any flavor is fine."

She sat in the family room, next to the window, trying to picture Reese running a hotel and being a trooper. No way could he manage that. Even if he could, there would be no room for quality time with his child, much less any time with her. God, she wished she could read minds. He'd been giving her mixed signals since they broke up. Then again, she'd probably been doing the same thing.

Reese put a tray of goodies on the coffee table,

then set her drink on a coaster. He left the room but returned with a bottle of red wine and one glass. He poured himself what most would consider two glasses.

"Seriously, how are you going to find the money to buy The Heritage Inn, much less run it?"

"There are a few things you don't know...that no one knows about me."

"That doesn't answer my question."

"My family is rich."

She sipped her flavored water, contemplating his words. *Rich.* And *family.* He'd never been cheap on their dates, always picking up the tab, but he lived like a poor man. At least, like someone who didn't have a whole lot of extra cash sitting around.

"How rich?"

He shrugged. "Like Richie Rich, rich." His eyes twinkled, but she could see he was serious. "My nana—"

"You have a nana? As in, a grandmother?"

He cracked a smile as he sat in the chair across from the window. That had always been his favorite spot. He said he liked looking at her profile while watching the sunset or sunrise. "I had a mother, too."

"Must you be so sarcastic? I feel like I don't know you at all."

"I'm sorry," he said. "It's weird for me to talk about it, especially the money part. When people think you have money, they treat you differently. I've never liked that."

She could understand that. Jared was rich, but he's always lived relatively modestly. People whispered and wondered, but no one knew. She supposed a few people did treat Jared differently, and a few people knew about his first wife. She was a gold digger, according to the gossip mills.

"Okay, so having a hard time grasping the idea that you actually have the funds to purchase The Heritage Inn, but it concerns me that the only reason you are doing it is because of the baby. I don't want you to feel trapped or tied down or obligated to do anything."

"Lots of things are going to be because of the baby. I'm okay with that. You gave me an out. I didn't take it."

He had a point. "Tell me about your nana. Are you close? Do you see her often?"

"She basically raised me. I see her three or four times a year. Call her once or twice a week. I'd say we're close."

"You've lived here for a couple of years. We've been sleeping together for months, and not once did you mention anything about a nana," Patty said. "Does she know about me?"

The way Reese dipped his gaze spoke volumes on where she stood in Reese's life, baby or no baby. "I've never talked to her about any woman I've dated."

"Why not?"

"She's a bit overprotective of me," Reese said, then sipped more wine. "I'm not being flip or mean, but until now, I haven't seen any point in telling anyone about her. But I'd like you to meet her."

Oy. That would be a lot to take, Patty thought. "Do you have siblings?"

"I'm an only child. My mother died when I was seventeen, but left my grandparents to raise me when I was seven. My father is in prison. He's not my biological father, but that's a long story."

"Prison?"

He nodded. "I didn't know until my mother was dying. Though he ran out on me and my mom when I was seven, so it was a shocker to find out: dad in prison, but not your dad."

"That sucks." So much of Reese made sense now

that it was impossible for her to ignore the longing in her heart.

"It did, for about five minutes. Living with Nana and Grandpa was great."

"Where is your grandpa now?"

"He passed away two years ago. Heart gave out. He was a real hard-ass sometimes, but a great man." The way Reese talked of his family, the slight tremble in his voice, was something she'd never heard, a deep, emotional connection filled with love and admiration.

Her heart ached for the little boy who'd been through so much, and for the man who carried that burden through his adult life. She wanted to ask him to join her on the sofa. To hold him. Feel his warm embrace. This couldn't be any easier for him to tell, than it was for her to listen. "I can't believe I didn't know any of this."

"Well, we did have that rule," he said. "Nothing personal."

"Does anyone know about any of this?"

"Jared knows a little."

"So, it wasn't just me you kept all this from?"

"It's not that I kept it from you, or anyone, but I didn't want to put it out there and make connections...because I tend to, as you know, not stay around very long."

"I'm still worried about that."

"I'm buying a hotel," he said. "I'm not going anywhere."

She studied his face, which had softened, his eyes less deep and secretive. Even the way he sat said he was open to the world.

But it was hard to trust. "I'm having a really hard time with that one."

"None of this changes who I am," he said. "I'm still the same person you've known the last few years."

"But it does." She shifted to face him. "Your secrets kept you from ever really being close to anyone. Even me, and we shared a bed for more than half a year. If it doesn't change who you are, then you're still the man who can't be in a long-term relationship."

"I see your point." He refilled his glass, took a healthy sip, then moved to the sofa and sat next her, which only added fuel to a fire that burned too hot. He smelled like a combination of brute masculinity and salt from the cool ocean air rolling in. He had a way of melting down all her defenses with a touch. When he looked at her, he focused on her every word. Her every move. Yet he'd never revealed himself. He'd managed to keep her just far enough away that sex was her only means of knowing him. He wasn't a talker, but he could listen. And he listened so well that before she was even finished talking, they were usually in bed.

"I don't know who you are at all, and you're telling me all this as if it's no big deal. What will happen in a few years when you get bored with being a trooper or running a hotel? Then what? What will happen to me? To your child? Are we just no big deal?"

"You're being melodramatic."

"You're being patronizing."

"Look." He put his arm around her and drew her close. "We need to spend some time getting to know one another again. Or rather, you, getting to know my history. I'm open to trying it out. Are you?"

Every instinct told her to push him away, but her heart told her to pull him closer and never let him go. She'd never experienced making love the way she had with him. With other men, it had been an act of affection, neither good nor bad. With Reese? Sex was empowering. Satisfying. Sometimes downright blush worthy dirty.

With Reese, making love came with no strings. It

was unabated and raw, and that gave her the ability to let her hair down and do things she'd only fantasized about. They never had to carry on real emotional or mentally challenging conversations, and she'd felt no sense of having to tell him anything, though she told him everything.

"I've already been open with you," she said. "There isn't much you don't know about me or my family."

"There is a lot I don't know about you." He inched closer. The warmth from his body flowed over to hers. "I don't know how you feel about a lot of things. The only thing I know for sure was that I was only meant to be a fling for you. You wanted nothing from me but a good time. You made that clear."

"So did you."

"We also said that when summer ended, we ended. We most certainly didn't end, and I'm not the one who ended it."

"You didn't do anything to keep it going."

They grew quiet for a long moment as Reese drained his glass and then poured the rest of the wine. He swirled it, and as she watched him, she realized that should have been a clue: his taste and knowledge of fine wines. The way he swirled it. Smelled it. Even once sent a bottle back.

She realized other things, too. Reese had always been the perfect gentleman. He never pushed. He was always respectful. She thought it had been some aspect of being a player, because he was smooth and women flocked to him.

But was it only that he was smooth, or just the way he grew up? Had his grandparents taught him manners? How to treat a lady?

She sank into the arm he'd wrapped around her shoulder. It felt safe. Comfortable. It felt normal to be here, like this, with him.

"We're having a baby," he whispered.

"Tell me something I don't know." She meant it rhetorically, so she was surprised but happy when he responded.

"My nana lives in White Plains. She's the only family I have, outside of you and this baby. If all goes as planned with The Heritage Inn, I want to bring her here, and I want us all to get along with whatever scenario we put forth, preferably one where you and I are more than what we are now."

"I don't know about that," she managed. She hadn't known what to expect when she told Reese about the baby, but this was not in even her wildest fantasies. "This is a lot to process."

"I understand," Reese said. "To be honest, the

night you told me about the baby, I was thinking about asking if we could pick things up again. I missed you. Then I had to go and act like some jerk."

"That you did." She let him pull her closer as he rubbed her shoulder with one hand and rested the other on her thigh. It felt natural and real. As though they fit together. She wondered if she should tell him about Keith Holland and his quiet inquiry into the property, but Reese had already made the offer. He was staying. For his child. She could live with that. "I missed you, too."

Her body, however, demanded so much more than comfortable, and right now, she just wanted him. Needed him. Not the closed-off Reese she'd been messing around with, but this Reese. The one who was going to be a father. She knew it was a bad idea.

Just one more time, she thought.

She cupped his face and kissed him on the lips, first slowly, gauging his response, then more passionately as he began to respond. Everything about their so-called relationship had been simple, yet so complicated for her. Once again, she found herself in the arms of a man who knew every single physical button to push.

Then he pulled away.

"Just for tonight," she said.

"I don't want it to be that way between us. I want to do this right this time."

"It's the way I need it to be right now."

His lips brushed against hers, teasingly.

She took his wine glass from his hand, placed it on the table, and then straddled him, holding his face, and looked deep into his eyes. She could see the passion, but she felt his trepidation. "We start over tomorrow," she said. "But tonight, I need this."

It didn't take long before they were naked in her bed, but there was no sense of urgency. He caressed every inch of her body. He kissed her shoulder. Licked her neck. Brushed his fingers across her breast as if she were a beautiful rose garden he tended to.

Desperate to have him inside her, she coaxed, but he resisted, taking his sweet time making sure every erogenous zone she had, and few she hadn't known she had, were fully engaged.

"Now," she begged.

"No," he whispered in her ear. "We start over tonight."

Her body and mind were wild with passion. She cared about nothing except the physical pleasure only he could give, that one last, noncommittal encounter. A way to end the physical and begin a friendship, but the way he touched her felt so different from anything she'd ever felt before. "Please," she begged again. "I need you."

Finally, he relented, entering her slowly, but she couldn't take it any longer. She needed release. She lifted her hips over and over until he gave up and matched her pace. "This is the beginning," he whispered.

After they were both fully satisfied, he rolled to his side, turning her, and held her close. He said nothing, just held her, wrapping both the blankets and his arms protectively around her. He'd always been one to enjoy a good cuddle after lovemaking, but she'd always kiss him, then push him away. Being held in his arms all night was against one of her rules during their so-called fling. A way to protect herself from falling too hard and too deep for a man who wasn't emotionally available.

The man who currently held her body close, his breathing slowing to a rhythmic sound of sleep, was someone completely different. She relaxed in his arms, letting sleep come. Dreams of what could be tickled her brain while she slept in the protective presence of the man she loved.

Chapter Five

Reese had a lot of reasons to be ashamed, but none more pressing than the fact he had skipped out on Patty this morning without so much as a gentle peck on the cheek. Nana would have called him a coward, and she'd be partially correct. Work had called him away, but he could have said goodbye instead of sneaking out in a walk of shame.

Last night wasn't supposed to happen. She was impossible to resist, and she had basically begged him, but that was no excuse.

He'd texted her, telling her he was sorry, duty called and all that. But all he got was one quick text back that read, *No worries*.

An unlikely response from Patty.

Reese felt Stacey kick him under the table. "Did you hear me?"

"Yeah," he said as he went through the paperwork once again. Most of it was straightforward. "Your dad is a good guy," Reese said.

"You can hire an outside attorney if you want to go over everything. My dad won't take it personally. It's business."

"I think I'll have Patty take a look at it, but I can sign the estimate as well as the paperwork to have them file everything."

"For now, that's all you need. Essentially, you're giving Sutten & Tanner permission to file for permits and variances, and naming Sutten & Tanner as the contractor for said work, and their plans as the intended construction, but nothing that bind either of you to each other right now."

"What I don't understand is why do we have to rush this?"

"In case anyone else is preparing to bid on the property, it shows your intention to the zoning board."

"Do you know if there are other interested buyers?"

"Rumor has it that Holland Development is

looking into various properties in the area, The Heritage Inn being one of them."

"That name sounds familiar." Reese signed the papers, except the work contract. He trusted it was all in order. He knew he was in good hands, but due diligence as his nana always told him.

"Big company with very deep pockets," she said. "He was actually at Conrad's office right before the altercation the other day."

"Why?"

"Conrad is his attorney of record, and also, the shooter was his employee."

"Excuse me? Why is this the first I'm hearing about this?"

"It wasn't relevant—"

"Anything to do with Patty is relevant for me to know," he said with a sharp tone as he shuffled the paperwork around on his desk, looking for the case file regarding the shooting. "So, the shooter used to work for this Holland guy, who might want to buy the property I'm putting a bid in on?" Well, that was interesting. That meant Patty had to have known about this other possible offer but didn't tell him. Maybe she couldn't. Attorney-client privilege and all. He pushed the paperwork for The Heritage Inn back in the envelope.

"Okay," Stacey said. "But it's not connected to Patty at all, or what happened. The guy was a past employee. Fired. Because of Conrad."

Reese nodded, blocking out the memoires of seeing Patty held at gunpoint by a crazy man. At the time, he hadn't known about the baby. But now that he did? It changed everything. "Do I need to drop these off?" He took in a deep breath, letting it out slowly. Patty and his baby were safe. They had a chance at a new beginning. It was time he make that his sole focus.

"My dad is on his way."

"That's nice of him," Reese said, still pushing papers around. He knew the file he wanted wouldn't be on his desk since he'd been the one who had shot the gunman.

"Yeah, that's my dad. Mr. Nice Guy. Now, I just need to find him a good woman."

Frank entered the station house, closing out his shift. "Kind of a boring day out there," he said as the main door flew open again.

"Hey, Daddy," Stacey said, greeting her father with a hug.

Jim stepped back and shook his head. "I still can't believe you carry a gun."

"I've had sex, too."

Jim closed his eyes and took in a long, deep breath. Reese figured raising that child had to be more than challenging.

"Reese," Jim said, his tone low. "Got the paperwork?"

"Yep." Reese handed Jim the envelope, forgetting Frank was even in the room. "You really think this land developer, Holland Development, could cause a problem with my offer?"

"I wish I could say no. All depends on if they put in an offer. I'm sure by now they know when your offer expires."

"What are you all talking about?" Frank asked.

Before Reese could cut Stacey off at the pass, she spilled the beans. "Reese just put in an offer to buy The Heritage Inn. Daddy is going to do all the—"

"You're joking, right? The man's broke."

"No, he's not," Stacey said. "As a matter of fact—"

"Now would be a good time for you to be quiet," Jim said. "And for me to leave. I'll be in touch." The station house remained quiet until after Jim closed the door behind him.

"How can you buy The Heritage Inn?" Frank asked. "Besides, didn't you put in for a transfer? Aren't you moving?"

"Redacted," Reese said. "I'm staying put."

Frank blinked a few times. "How in the hell can you afford to buy it?"

"Well, let's just say my family has a bit of money."

"What family?" Frank asked.

"My nana."

"You have a nana?"

"Most people have grandparents." Reese smiled. He could have some fun with this letting people in on shit, just to see their reactions. Even Stacey gave him an odd look, like they all thought wolves had raised him.

"The asking price on that place is over six mil." Frank's contorted expression was priceless. "It makes no sense at all. And why? Can't do that and be a trooper at the same time."

"Yeah, Reese. How is that possible? And why are you doing that? I mean, putting down roots and all?" Jared asked, and by the look on his face, he was enjoying adding fuel to the fire. So much for worrying about the drama in the office.

"Not important," Reese said. "But you all are going to have to get used to my ugly mug around here, because I'm not going anywhere."

"Then let's get back to work," Jared said, half

laughing.

Frank sat at his desk, filling out his paperwork. "None of my business," he said. "But you spent the night at Patty's place. Are the two of you back together?"

"You're right, none of your business." Reese snagged the keys to the patrol car and nodded to Stacey to follow.

"For someone who says he's not relationship material," Frank yelled, his tone teasing. "You seem to be unable to end a relationship with my cousin." Reese just waved and left the station. It was going to take some getting used to living in a small town where everyone knows everything about everyone.

"You're fired."

Patty hadn't expected those words when her boss stormed into her office.

"Excuse me?" she managed.

"You heard me," Conrad said. "Pack your things and leave now."

"Why, exactly?"

Conrad pressed both fists against her desk, leaning forward. His eyes were laced with anger and sadness, and perhaps something else, but Patty was too stunned to try to figure it out.

"You've botched The Heritage Inn sale," Conrad said.

"How have I done that?" She also wanted to ask what sale, because last she heard their client hadn't settled on any one property.

"You were there yesterday with a different prospective buyer who, rumor has it, is your boyfriend. Right after you were in a private meeting with our clients, who were interested in that property. That's a conflict of interest, one of which should have been handled before it happened. I'd also say that was grounds for firing."

"I see," Patty said. "For the record, I was blind-sided last night by a friend." Not that it was any of Conrad's business. "He put in the offer before I even showed up. I told him nothing of our client or his possible intent."

"Seems like too much of a coincidence to me," Conrad said, "and our client is quite upset. So upset that if I don't fire you, he will take his business else-where." That explained Conrad's tortured face.

"So, he wants me fired..." She paused for a moment. "I told you first thing this morning that an offer had been made, which you already knew, because the real-estate agent told you. That said, the property is not sold yet." But Conrad was right; it was now officially a conflict of interest. "I get that keeping me on the case might be troublesome, since the other buyer is a friend. You could always move this case to Ben or Russ. Better yet, hire a temp. We could use the help, and I'll just stay clear of it."

"I could do that," Conrad said, "but Holland is insistent that I fire you."

"I'm sorry," she said. "I need this job. Firing me isn't the answer." She thought about mentioning the baby and needing insurance, but before she could open her mouth, Conrad slid papers across her desk. He frowned, looking as if he were truly sorry. "Severance package. And it's a good one. I think it's for the best."

"Could I at least talk with Mr. Holland?" Patty was dumbfounded. Conrad was always the kind of man who looked for a solution before pulling the trigger.

"I'd take the severance package," a voice echoed from behind Conrad. "The moment the offer went in, you should have notified me."

"It was late when I found out," Patty said. "I notified Conrad first thing this morning." She still felt guilty about it. She wanted Reese to have The

Heritage Inn if he wanted it, but he hadn't told her in confidence, so she felt obligated to tell her employer.

"A little too late," Keith Holland said. "We had to find out when we put in our offer. Had we known, we would have sweetened our deal a little more."

Patty looked into Holland's eyes, the color identical to Reese's, but the depth was quite different. She shivered. "I need this job, and I did nothing wrong."

"All right," Keith said. "Get your friend to redact his offer, you keep your job."

Patty was too stunned to utter anything. She sat there, hands on her desk, as the blood running through her veins began to burn with fury.

Keith and Conrad stepped out of the office. She couldn't hear their whispered conversation, but Keith didn't look thrilled. Five minutes passed before they returned to her office.

Keith smiled. "I do want to make it clear that I have every intention of buying The Heritage Inn." He pushed a card across her desk. "Talk to your friend. Ask him what it will take," he said.

"I don't—"

"Just ask him," Keith insisted. "If he's still hell-bent on buying, then it would be a conflict of interest for you to continue, so Conrad will then fire you, and you'll get the severance package he offered." Keith smiled widely. His eyes lowered, then came back up to catch her gaze as he leaned over her desk. There was nothing pleasant about this man at all. "You have until tomorrow, and in your condition and being single, I think this job would be top priority. So get it done."

As soon as she saw them turn the corner toward the conference room, she realized she'd been holding her breath. She let the air out in one quick whoosh. Her hands trembled, and her pulse pounded like a drum inside her head. It was a subtle threat. But a threat nonetheless.

And how did he know about the baby?

Every little noise in the apartment set Patty on edge. She resented it, and probably should have told Reese to come over right away instead of waiting for his shift to end.

She shook off the negative feeling and continued to search through current town records. If an offer was accepted, it would show up pretty quickly. A counter wouldn't show up, but when she called

Charlie's office, she got voicemail, so she left a message. She'd called a distant relative on the zoning committee. He only knew rumor and rumblings. She pulled up the deed and the title, noting the changes over the years. Any request to change the current land configuration, including height and placement of buildings, would require all sorts of variances that every homeowner in this area would fight.

The sun had started to set behind the mountains, and even though the night air was cooler, she felt spring approaching. April was an odd month, swinging between warmth and snow. Some days, boaters would enjoy temperatures approaching fifty. Other days, it snowed, and only the diehard fishermen braved the unforgiving, freezing lake.

The doorbell disrupted her thoughts. She checked the time. Reese was early.

She walked down to the lower alcove, slowing down as she saw it wasn't Reese, but a girl with a large bouquet of flowers.

No one ever sent her flowers. Ever. Black-thumb Harmon had been her nickname ever since she'd single-handedly managed to kill a cactus and then an Aloe Vera plant. Reese knew about her inability to keep any plant alive. He'd teased her about it, so he wouldn't send her flowers.

"Patty Harmon?" the delivery girl asked.

"Yes."

"These are for you." The young woman handed her a basket filled with flowers, or maybe plants, since it was in a pot of dirt, but it was blooming. Patty had no idea. But Reese would know, and she always found it odd that Reese knew and enjoyed everything about gardening. When he'd moved into Lacy's trailer, the first thing he had done was put in flowering bushes and an herb garden. And Reese was an excellent cook. Another thing that Patty wasn't very good at, though, she gave herself an A for effort.

"Thanks." Patty put the large arrangement on the floor, then plucked out the card.

Make it happen—Keith.

The veiled threat left her unnerved.

"Who are those from?" Reese kicked off his boots in the alcove.

Before she could snag the card and the flowers and head back up to her apartment, Reese snatched the card right out of her hands.

"Who's Keith, and make what happen?" A hint of jealousy lingered in his voice, and she kind of enjoyed it.

"Keith is the reason I asked you to stop by."

He stopped in the middle of the steps. "Do I need to be worried about this Keith guy?"

"Yes, and maybe no."

"I don't like the sound of that," he said.

"Reese McGinn, are you jealous? Because it sounds like you're a little jealous."

"Yep," he said. "Got any lunch meat?" he asked. "I'm starving. Haven't eaten all day."

"Help yourself."

She put the flowers on the table in the family room and waited for Reese. Might as well let the man have his food since he was always cranky when hungry.

He sauntered in from the kitchen carrying a plate in one hand with a very thick sandwich, turkey and ham flowing over the sides, and a beer in the other. He sat on the floor, resting everything on the coffee table. "So, tell me about the guy who is sending the mother of my baby flowers, and why I shouldn't be jealous, but it has you upset." No sooner did he say the words than he stuffed his mouth. She liked this playful, more engaged side of Reese. He'd always been fun, but never with any depth to it, no real emotions. Just gentlemanly gestures, and while valued, they weren't loving. Sitting with him right now, she felt loved by him. He was a tad jealous, but he had no reason to be, and that concept made her heart flutter with affection. With hope of what could be.

More importantly, he was upset.

Let's backtrack. "Conrad tried to fire me today."

"Why would he do that?"

"Because Keith told him to."

"And who is this Keith guy to Conrad?

"Keith Holland—"

"As in Holland Development?" Reese put half his sandwich on the plate. "The owner of Holland Development is sending you flowers?"

"Someone saw us at the Heritage, and Mr. Holland thinks I gave you the heads-up that he was thinking about buying the place."

"But you never told me a thing. Want me to go talk to them? Really, that's ridiculous."

"Thanks," she said. "But there is only one way I'll get my job back, and that's if I can convince you to take back your offer. That's what he meant by 'Make it happen' on the card."

"And you agreed?" His tone remained even, but laced with a hint of hurt.

"I didn't disagree," she said. "He didn't threaten me, but it felt like a threat, so I opted to say nothing and come home. Tomorrow, I'll tell them I couldn't, and I'll be out of a job."

"This happened when you asked me to come over." He glanced at his Apple Watch. "What, over four hours ago, and you're just telling me now? When did the flowers come?"

"Two minutes before you showed up."

Reese hoisted himself off the floor, then joined her on the sofa. "What, exactly, did he say that made you feel threatened?"

"It wasn't what he said as much as what he implied. He said a woman in my condition, being single, would need the income from regular employment, so get it done."

"He knows you're pregnant? You told Conrad?"

She shook her head. "That's what freaked me out. The only people who I've told are you and Lacy. No one else knows."

"That's not entirely true." Reese rubbed his hand across his head. "Jared knows."

"You told Jared?"

"I might have told a few other people that night I found out and got shit-faced at the Mason Jug."

"Oh, shit." She closed her eyes. "So, everyone in my family probably knows and is wondering why I haven't told them."

"Sorry about that," he said. "But let's stick to what Conrad and this Holland guy said. If you get me to back off, you get your job. What if I don't?"

"I get a good severance package."

"So, not really a deadly threat, but definitely implied pressure, and totally unfounded," Reese said. "They can't fire you for something you didn't do. Really, it's ridiculous. You should hire a lawyer."

"I work for a lawyer," she said. "Honestly, it was so hard being back there. They covered Matt's blood with a floor mat. I can't relive that day constantly, but I need the insurance."

"I'll take care of that," he said.

"I don't want your money."

"Okay, it's not for you, it's for our baby. Your need for health insurance is for the benefit of our baby, and if that asshole is going to fire you and I can't make you fight it, then you have to at least let me pay for that. Can I do that?"

She bit back a giggle. She could get used to this Reese. "Yes," she said, but her relief was quickly squashed. "There's something about Mr. Holland I don't like...and the guy that shot Matt used to work for Holland."

"We're on the same page about that." Reese leaned forward, resting one hand on his knee, the other rubbing his neck. She knew that pose, and it frightened her. "We're still doing background checks on that guy. Seems Conrad found out he was skimming off a construction site, and Holland fired Terry—the perp who broke into your office and held you captive."

"Holland said he'd never met the guy."

"Possible, in a large company like that, but for now"—Reese wrapped his arm around her and pulled her in tight, leaning back on the sofa—"just tell them I wouldn't back down, take the severance package, and don't look back."

She raised her feet onto the sofa and rested her head on his chest. Things were different. And that was good. She wasn't ready to go full-swing, but this was nice, a start in the right direction. "Who the hell is going to hire a pregnant woman?"

"You'll find a job," he said. "Come to think of it, I'll need a manager for the hotel."

"I'm a paralegal, but thanks for the offer." She tilted her head and looked into his eyes. "This is nice, but don't go getting ideas."

"Too late." He kissed her softly.

"Slow. As in we date. Like real dating."

"I guess that means I'm not sleeping here tonight."

"Nope."

A pounding at the door startled them both. It was Frank, and he looked none too happy.

"What are you doing here?" Patty asked. "Don't you have that thing with Andy?"

"Something came up," Frank said. His tone indicated that whatever suddenly came up was pretty unpleasant. She also sensed it was about her. "I see that Reese is here, so I can kill two birds with one stone."

"What does that mean?" Reese asked.

"I know Patty's pregnant. The whole town knows, thanks to your drunken ass." He turned to Reese. "I was fine with it until I found out what a total asshole you are." His voice was eerily even, though the words cut through the air with a dark edge.

"He's one of your best friends," Patty said. "Why would you say that?"

Frank turned to Patty, taking an envelope out of his coat pocket. He looked only at Patty. His lips pursed, and he clenched the envelope in his hands with such anger it flowed through the room like the wind ripping in off the lake.

"He's not the stand-up guy I thought he was." Frank held up his hand when Patty opened her mouth. "As a matter of fact, he's a lying bastard and has had us all snowed." Frank shook his head, his eyes closed and his fists balled tight. He opened his eyes. They were on fire, but there was something else that flickered behind that rage, and Patty recognized it immediately. Betrayal. "I was okay with this until I found out who that man really is. If Reese had been honest up front, things would be different, but he's a liar and not worthy of you or that child."

"What the fuck are you talking about?" Reese asked.

Frank handed the envelope to Patty. "He's never been honest with you, and I'm not sure he would have told you about this, ever."

Reese stepped a few feet closer. "What are you talking about?"

Patty ignored the two men yelling at each other while she opened the contents of the envelope. There was one picture and one document, but they spoke a thousand words. "Where did you get this?"

"It was delivered by messenger to the station today," Frank said.

"What is it?" Reese reached for the papers, but she jerked them back, looking at them again. Tears rolled down her cheeks.

"It's your marriage license," Frank said. "And your wedding picture."

Patty's heart sank. She blinked a few times, but the words on the document didn't change. Nor did the picture of Reese all decked out in a tux next to some redhead.

And what was worse, Reese just stood there, shock registering on his face, then slowly turning into shame. He looked like a man who knew he was busted, and there was no point in trying to deny it. Guilty as charged, but only because he was caught.

"So it's true," she whispered. Her voice trembled. This was worse than when her mother had left. Her best friend had just stabbed her in the back.

"Bastard," Frank yelled, inching closer to Reese.

"Who sent these to you?" Reese didn't back down, the look of shame turning to a rage she'd never seen on him, and it was beyond horrifying.

"No idea," Frank said. "But someone who gives a shit about Patty, unlike you."

"Both of you shut up," Patty said, but Frank lunged toward Reese with a right hook.

Reese's head snapped to the side and he stumbled back, tripping over the ottoman, knocking over the lamp, then finally landing on the floor. He wiped his lip, now split and bloodstained. "You should have come to me first," Reese said. "Let me explain."

Patty pushed in front of Frank as he was about to hoist Reese off the floor and most likely hit him again. "I need you to leave." She held Frank's shoulders, feeling them tremble with rage. "I appreciate your defense, but I need to talk to Reese alone."

"I'm not leaving you with this lying, cheating bastard."

"Yes. You are." Patty escorted Frank to the door, leaving Reese on the floor to lick his wounds. She hated to admit it, but considering the recent turn of events, she was glad Frank had punched him. Though she still considered giving him a good sucker punch in the gut, but not until after she told him exactly where he could go.

"I'll be right downstairs."

"Thanks." She closed the door and watched Frank until he disappeared into his apartment before unleashing her own rage on the father of her baby.

Chapter Six

"You're fucking married?"

Reese wasn't sure if he'd ever heard Patty drop the F-bomb before. The words echoed in his ears, cutting straight to his aching heart. He had hoped to take care of the situation before having to tell her anything of his sham of a marriage. Then again, she probably would have reacted just as she was right now.

He hoisted himself to the ottoman, feeling a trickle of blood roll down his chin. He wiped it with his sleeve. He had managed to collect the license and wedding picture from Patty. He'd had his reservations about marrying Jessica. Hours' worth of lectures from Grandpa and Nana about her being a gold-digging hussy had been painful to hear, because part of him thought it was true. The day he married her, his grandparents changed their wills, leaving him nothing. That same day, they tore up those wills.

Nana was going to have his head.

"Jessica—"

"I take it that's your wife's name." Bitterness dripped from her words, far more painful than Frank's punch.

He nodded. "It's not what—"

"I'm sure it's exactly what I think," she said.

He knew he didn't deserve any compassion from her. And maybe telling her the truth wouldn't garner any, either. But it was time to put all his cards on the table. "I married her because she was pregnant—"

"That does not help," she said. "Please don't tell me you have a child out there somewhere who you never see."

"Jessica never had the baby." Reese sat on the edge of the ottoman, dabbing the blood from his chin. The moment he walked out on Jessica, he'd never looked back. He got over the pain and shock, and eventually he stopped thinking about her altogether.

But he never forgot what she had done.

He looked up at Patty. She stood in front of the picture window, her back turned.

"Did she miscarry?"

"I met Jessica when I returned from my first tour in the Middle East, when my mother was dying. I was barely twenty years old." He paused, waiting for any kind of reaction. He got nothing. "I was young and stupid, and more importantly, angry."

"About what?"

"About having been lied to about who my father was," he said. "My mother had been in and out of my life for years, leaving Nana and Grandpa to take care of me. I was already resentful of my mother, but her last words cut deep. She said the man I called Dad was in federal prison, serving two life sentences for murder, and my real father would have been worse. She slipped into a coma and died a few days later."

"That's cruel."

"It was," Reese said.

"What does this have to do with your wife?" Patty's tone was as cruel as his mother's words. Only this time, he deserved it.

"Jessica was a waitress at a bar where I met the PI I hired to find my real father. *If* there was any truth to the story my mother told."

"Didn't your nana know?" She still refused to look at him.

"She said she had no idea. I did a paternity test, and sure enough, Allen McGinn was not my father."

"Did your dad…Allen…know?"

"That he wasn't my father? I don't know. I guess so. I visited him once after my mother died. He didn't have much to say, just that he was sorry for everything."

Patty finally turned, briefly made eye contact, and then sat on the sofa, where she stared at her thumbs as she twirled them on her lap. "I can see this deeply affected you, but I still don't know what it has to do with the fact you are married, or why you never told me, especially after I told you about the baby. Especially after last night. More importantly, that you married a woman just because she was pregnant."

"For two months, Jessica was always there when I needed her. I thought I was in love with her, so when she told me she was pregnant we got married. It seemed like the right thing to do at the time."

Patty snapped her head up. "Like sticking around here, being all honorable because of a baby."

He shook his head. "I was thinking about sticking around here before I knew about our baby. I was just too scared, and you didn't seem to want me anymore."

"Don't put all that on me."

"I'm not."

"So, how long after she lost the baby did you run out on her?"

"She didn't have a miscarriage. Nana hated Jessica and thought we were moving way too fast, and after everything with my mother, Nana hired her own investigators who, about six hours after we'd gotten married, let me know at my wedding reception that a week before the wedding, Jessica had terminated the pregnancy." He closed his eyes, remembering that day more vividly than he wanted to. When he had confronted Jessica, she accused his grandmother of doctoring the records, but Nana would never stoop that low.

"I'm sorry. I really am. It doesn't change the fact that you chose not to tell me. That hurts."

"I've never understood why Jessica did it. Aborted our baby before our wedding, and still married me. I never asked. I volunteered for another tour of duty, and that was that. I never looked back. Until now."

Patty went green, then raced to the bathroom. It

was a small apartment, so he could easily hear her vomiting.

The only other person that knew, besides Jessica, had been his nana and her investigators, but no one ever talked about it. The few times Nana had brought Jessica up, the details had always been buried so deep he couldn't allow what Jessica had done to their child to surface.

Bile hit the back of his throat with such force that his only recourse was to punch the wall. He left a small dent in the drywall, and now blood speckled his knuckles, but the action didn't alleviate the sense of dread he felt. He should have told Patty a long time ago.

"You're going to pay for that." Patty stood behind him, her hands on her hips.

"I suspect I will," he said. "Are you okay?"

She nodded. "I suppose morning sickness of some kind."

He supposed the shock of his confession just made her ill. "I've never told anyone about Jessica before."

"No one?" She touched his arm, a soft touch that could have meant anything or nothing, and yet it meant everything to him.

He shook his head. "I did another tour of active

duty, but Nana drove me nuts with her worry, so a year later, I came back and became a cop and started making my way through various stations. She still drives me nuts, but she worries less."

"I'm so very sorry about what Jessica did," Patty said. "But it doesn't excuse not telling me."

"I know."

She laced her fingers through his and drew him back into the family room. "I understand a lot more about who you are, that's for sure." Her words were soft and tender.

"I should have divorced her years ago." He was grateful to sit on the sofa next to Patty, holding her hand, feeling her thumb caress his rough skin. They had something. Something special, and he was going to make it right. "I avoided it because I can't stand to think about her or what she did to our... Well, I can't change what she did."

"No, you can't," Patty said. "So, where is this wife now?"

He shrugged. "I have no idea, but I hired someone to try to find her. This guy Brad. You might remember him from Lacy's case. Nana is also checking in with her family to see if they still live in New Jersey."

"This is a lot to process."

"I'm not going anywhere," he said, pulling her in closer, resting his head on top of hers, smelling the fresh melon scent from her shampoo.

"I believe you. Still need time to process." She ended the embrace long before he was ready to let go. If he was being honest, he never wanted to let her go. The knowledge he'd just broken her heart put a pain in his gut that he wasn't sure he'd ever be able to get rid of. "Why don't we have dinner or something tomorrow?" she asked.

"That sounds nice."

"I'll talk to you then."

He nodded, letting things settle into perspective and feeling better. Now, on to deal with this Holland asshole, and divorce his wife.

With only one boot on, he flew down the stairs, two at a time. He wasn't surprised to find Frank waiting by the door, arms down by his sides, but puffed out like a rooster ready to fight.

"I should beat the shit out of you," Frank said.

"Probably," Reese agreed. "But we need to set that aside, because Keith Holland—"

"I don't give a shit about your stupid hotel."

"Shut up and listen to me." Reese shook his head. "Holland put the squeeze on Patty. Threatened her, without threatening her."

"What do you mean?"

"Conrad tried to fire her. Holland gave her a day to change my mind about buying the hotel."

"And if she doesn't?"

"She gets fired. He made an implied threat about her 'condition,'" Reese said. "So, can you put aside your anger for five minutes and help me figure out how to connect all this? Because if that Terry guy was slimy, I bet his former boss is worse."

"We haven't identified any connection other than working for Holland Development, which is a huge company. Holland didn't even know that guy."

Reese arched a brow.

"Okay," Frank said. "I get it, but once we figure that out, I'm going to use you for a punching bag."

"I'm sure there will be a long line of people waiting to follow your lead."

Chapter Seven

"What did you find out from the FBI?" Jared asked.

"They're looking into Holland," Reese said. "But they won't fill me in. Something about how it's not a State matter."

"My contact at the State Attorney's Office," Stacey said. "She has a different perspective. They tried to build a case against Holland a few years ago and came up way short, but he's always on their radar."

"Who is your contact?" Jared asked.

"A classmate from undergrad," Stacey said. "Her name is Bethany Ingrid, and she's sending us everything she can, which isn't much. I've been able to pull tons of information about Holland and his employee, Terry. It's all printing now. I'll share it when it's done."

"Wow," Reese said. "The little girl has contacts. Impressive."

"You don't want to be pushing my buttons," Stacey said. "I know all about your little wife, and I think Frank over there should have done more than split your lip."

"This is not the place," Jared said. "I don't want any personal crap brought in here. It happens again, someone will be taking a long leave, got it?"

"Yes, sir," Stacey said.

"Frank?" Jared asked.

"I'm good."

Reese nodded. He knew Frank was still pissed, but he also knew that Patty had given him the entire story. Not all was forgiven, but the emotions were less raw, and they agreed to put any personal shit on hold until all this stuff had been cleared up.

"That's really weird," Stacey said as she compiled some of the paperwork Jared's secretary had brought her.

"What?" Jared asked.

"Nothing, just that Reese sort of looks like Holland. The chin is the same. So are the eyes, well, the color, not so much the shape."

"No, I don't," Reese said, but Stacey held up the picture and the resemblance floored him. It was subtle, but it was there. "I guess I do." He looked between the two pictures, noting the similarities, then focused on the differences.

"Everyone has a twin," Stacey said. "I'm always told I look like Kelly Ripa."

"You do," Reese said. For some reason, that knowledge made him feel better.

"Let's get back on track," Jared said. "So Terry had been picked up a few times, but never convicted. What were the charges, and how did they get dropped so quickly?"

"Robbery, first degree," Reese said. "And it looks like a high-priced attorney got all the charges dropped each time."

"Who's the attorney?" Jared asked.

"Someone at Baker, Wolowitz, Ramond, and Healy," Reese said. "A large firm out of New York City, with a satellite office in Albany."

"That's the firm that Doug's wife works for," Stacey said.

"Can you ask her about Terry, and why their firm handled it?" Reese asked.

"Not sure she'll tell me anything."

"Go in uniform," Jared said. "Make it seem official."

"I'm not going to scare her, but I'll see what I can find out."

"So, I've got a question," Frank said. "Why is someone like Holland using a local attorney for The Heritage Inn deal? I'm sure he's got some big, fancy lawyer that handles all this for him on other projects."

"Yeah, Baker, Wolowitz, Ramond, and Healy," Jared added. "Let's take this in the big room."

The big room was where they kept the whiteboard, blackboard, and corkboard for working major cases. They currently had none, and this technically wasn't one yet. Jared and Stacey pinned up pictures of all the players, or if they didn't have a picture, they wrote the names. On the whiteboard, they diagrammed how those players were connected. They used the chalkboard for theories that could be adjusted or deleted as they moved through the case.

Right now, there were no theories.

Reese straddled one of the chairs and studied the boards. Frank leaned against the doorjamb, arms folded, deep in thought. Stacey and Jared stood to the side, hands on their hips, staring at the board.

"So," Stacey said, surprising Reese with her

initiative as she jumped right in. "Terry worked for Holland Development in construction." She pulled out a file. "He worked there with a clean record for ten years. Three years ago, a building he supervised construction on had some issues, and people got hurt. He was suspended for six months, then brought back on, then fired because—and this is where it gets interesting—Winston and Associates found some issues with the accounting on one of the sites. It appears Terry was pulling a fast one and pocketing some money."

"The interesting part," Reese said. "Just to clarify, Winston and Associates is our one and only Conrad, right?"

Stacey nodded. She flipped through other paperwork. "Holland does use Mary's firm, but not the Albany office. He uses the one in New York City. It appears Conrad does subcontract work for the satellite office, which wouldn't be that unusual, except the construction site was downstate."

"That is interesting," Frank said.

"That still doesn't give us a big enough common denominator," Reese said. "There are logical explanations to all these connections, except the high-priced attorney getting Terry out of community service or a year in jail."

"I'll go check into that now," Stacey said. "Reese, you want to ride shotgun?"

He laughed. "You're still sitting passenger, little girl."

Just as they left the big room, the doors to the station opened. Not many people walked into the trooper station out of the blue, so it was a shock to see Keith Holland, with his hauntingly similar eyes, enter the building with his entourage.

"Is a Reese McGinn here?" Keith Holland said.

"That's me." Reese stepped forward. "What can I do for you?" He noticed that Frank and Stacey maneuvered toward the front desk and pretended to look over a file together. Jared leaned over the secretary's desk.

"Is there a place we can talk privately?"

"Not really. And you are...?" Reese knew exactly who stood in front of him, but he wasn't going to let him know that.

"Keith Holland of Holland Development, and you and I find ourselves in a bit of a predicament."

"How is that?"

Keith smiled as he looked around the station, taking in the bland ambience while he took off his gloves, finger by finger. Reese knew he meant to intimidate, with his legs spread shoulder-width and the way he carried himself.

Not many people could intimidate Reese, and Keith Holland was not one of them. Even with his hauntingly similar eyes.

"I'd prefer to do this in private. Do you have an office?"

Reese held his arms open. "This is my office, and I've got to get out on patrol, so unless this is a matter of police business, which our desk officer can discuss with you, I suggest you let me know what this is about."

Holland closed the gap. Reese figured Holland expected him to take a few steps backward, so Reese instead met him halfway.

"I have a business proposition for you." Holland smiled as if he'd just solved the world's problems.

"And what is that?"

"I'll pay you twice your offer if you back away from the Heritage deal."

"I don't want money," Reese said. "I have plenty of that. I do, however, want that hotel, so thanks, but no thanks."

"I find it fascinating that a state trooper would want to run a hotel. You know what I'd like to do with the property?"

"Build condos," Reese retorted.

Holland laughed. "My dear boy, of course not. I'm looking to make this my summer home. Bring my family. My children. My grandchildren. You see, I'm not getting any younger, and I want to slow down and spend time with what's really important in life. I suspect you can understand that." He leaned in and whispered, "I think you should consider my offer. It will be beneficial to both of us."

Reese leaned in and whispered back, "I'm glad you finally manned up, instead of threatening a young woman."

"I didn't threaten anyone," Holland said. "I'm just saying the offer will expire at the end of today. I've got deep pockets, son. I know yours don't run as deep. This is a battle you don't want. It's a battle I don't want. I just want to spend time with my family, that's all."

And with that, Holland turned on his very expensive heel, then walked out the door, his entourage in tow.

"Well, that was exciting," Stacey said.

Reese shook out his hands. He had to admit, he did sort of look like that guy, so he was creepy, as well as threatening.

"That man has balls," Jared said.

"I suspect he's got a big prick to go with those balls," Frank added.

"I'd hate to hear what you'd say if that were a woman waltzing in here like that, spouting off crap like that," Stacey said.

"Little girl," Jared said. "Let's just say even you would blush." Jared tapped Stacey's nose. "Now, go out there and find me some connections, and just maybe I'll admit to changing your diaper."

"You've got a deal."

"I knew having her here would be weird," Frank muttered.

She might add an odd element to the station house, but it was also refreshing. "All right, little girl, let's go," Reese said.

Chapter Eight

Patty dumped the boxes from her aunt's house at the top of the stairs. Baby stuff.

"Need a hand?" Lacy said from the bottom of the stairs.

"I'm good."

"Want to come down and talk?"

"Actually, I do." Patty kicked a box into her hallway, then headed back down with a heavy heart. This should have been a time of joy and hope, but she felt only confusion and trepidation. All she wanted was to bring a child into a happy and healthy environment. She wanted Reese to be part of the environment. The wife was an issue, and Patty still wasn't sure how Reese really felt about her. He was opening up, but being honest didn't equal being in love.

"Frank told me about your situation with the job." Lacy held up a bottle of red wine. "Mind if I have a drink?"

"Just because I'm pregnant doesn't mean everyone else has to be dry too."

"He also told me Reese was married."

Bad news traveled fast. "Yeah, that came as a shocker, and I have no idea what to do with it. We'd been getting along so well. He was opening up, and we were enjoying each other. Almost like a couple, but then, bam, 'Oh, by the way, I'm married.'" Patty sank into the plush leather sofa. Lacy's family room didn't overlook the lake, but it had a nice view of thick, lush pine trees. The lights from the cars on Route 9 flickered against the snow-dusted trees as the moon cast its eerie glow. "It's not even that he's been married, or even still married, though that is pretty icky...but he had so many chances to tell me. I don't understand why he didn't, especially since he's hell-bent on us living under the same roof."

"From what Frank told me, it seems Reese just wanted to brush it all under the rug, and I guess I can't blame him. Pretty cold, what his wife did."

"You should have seen the look on his face when he told me. I can tell he loved that baby, even when the baby no longer existed. It was heart-wrenching.

But I have a hard time forgiving him for not telling me he was married. It makes me wonder what other secrets he has that he's not sharing, and that's no way to start a relationship."

"Frank was so hurt about the fact Reese was married that he never even got a chance to be happy about you and the baby. And he really is happy for you."

"Frank has the biggest man-crush on Reese, it's almost gross," Patty said.

A long silence filled the room. It wasn't uncomfortable. Lacy had become more than her cousin's wife. She'd become Patty's best friend. Her confidant. Her sister from another mother, so to speak. She could say anything to Lacy, or not say anything, and they'd work through it. Lacy was always honest and upfront. Patty admired that, even when it hurt her feelings or she disagreed. Negative feelings between them never lasted.

"I feel like Reese and I can't move forward until this marriage thing is cleared." Patty tucked her feet up under her. She sipped her water as she stared at the electric fireplace.

"Nothing you can do until he finds her and takes care of it. I know he's using department resources, and I guess the Sutten girl has a few contacts helping with the search. It's only a matter of time."

"I'm worried something else from his past is going to reach out and derail me again."

"He's totally changed this last year. We were all a little surprised you broke up. It was kind of obvious Reese had it bad for you."

"You're kidding, right?" Patty asked.

"No. Frank said he'd changed the second he started dating you."

"I don't know," Patty said. "Between knowing about his family, a wife, and being rich, I'm just overwhelmed. I thought the man I was sleeping with just wanted a life with no ties. No commitments. The freedom to move about the world the moment he got bored. I could have lived with him being a part-time dad. I didn't bargain for a millionaire buying a hotel, and oh, by the way, he's married— but he wants to make it work with me. That's not the man I was sleeping with."

"Actually..." Lacy turned to face Patty, the moon shining through the window, dancing in her blond hair. She was not only beautiful, but she was confi-dent, and it showed. "That is exactly the man you were sleeping with. You knew he had secrets. A past. That he was emotionally unavailable. Broken, even.

You just didn't know the why. Now you know the why."

"That doesn't make this any easier. I feel like he's reacting, and not acting."

"How do you mean?"

"He tells me things only when he has to."

Andy barreled through the door. "Turn on the news!"

"Well, hello, to you, too," Lacy said. "And you can say hello to Aunt Patty as well."

"Hello, Aunt Patty," Andy said. "But seriously, turn on the news."

"The news isn't on right now," Lacy said. "Why don't you tell us about the art project you've been working on with your friend for the—"

"There's a fire at the trailer park. The one we used to live in," Andy yelled. "You know, the one Reese lives in now!"

Reese closed the ambulance door. One of the few neighbors who lived in the trailer park year-round, and in the winter for hunting or ice fishing, was tucked away inside with minor burns and a possible broken arm. The ambulance's siren blipped a couple of times as it pulled out onto Route 9. Reese sat on a rock and looked out over the smoldering wreckage of what used to be his new toy and his home. Fire-fighters were still on scene, working closely with the investigators.

Jared and Frank huddled under a tree, farther away from the wreckage. The moon shone brightly through the leafless branches, highlighting the smoke lingering in the air. The lead investigator had joined Frank and Jared, but Reese simply couldn't make his body move. Had he not decided to meet Jim and Doug for a beer to celebrate his offer's acceptance, he might have been home when this happened.

There had been two distinct fires. One had started in Reese's trailer, and one in his Mustang. It could have been worse. Only three other trailers had been damaged. Only one of them had a current occupant.

Thankfully, no one was killed.

Jared strolled over to Reese, then joined him on another rock.

"We should get some marshmallows," Reese said.

"Good to have a sense of humor." Jared's tone indicated he didn't share it. "Neighbor said he saw someone smoking behind the trailer."

Reese had just bought that Mustang not two months ago. It was a 1966 pale-blue convertible in mint condition. The thing purred like a kitten. He looked around the park at the damage. "Did you know my offer to buy the Heritage was accepted?"

"I did know that," Jared said. "Kind of puts a new perspective on this situation."

Frank made his way to the clearing and took a seat next to Jared. The three men sat in silence. The other law enforcement officials, investigators, and firefighters still on the premises were taking statements from the few people who dared to live in a trailer park in Hague during the brutal upstate winters.

"This fire went up too quickly," Reese commented.

"A lot of things could have caused it to get out of control," Jared said without any real conviction, and he had the same look on his face that Reese felt in his gut.

This was no accident.

Reese looked around the area and noted the lead arson investigator, Harrison Jakel, was poking around what remained of the Mustang. Harrison barked out a few orders, and someone else rushed over. Reese didn't know the other guy, but the two men hunched over something, pointed, and nodded. Harrison rose, then headed for Reese.

He stood in anticipation. So did Jared and Frank.

"Sergeant McGinn?" Harrison asked.

"Yes."

"Real sorry about what happened here."

"Thanks."

Harrison was only about five foot eight, but he was broad and prematurely gray for a man who was only in his late thirties. "We don't have much to go on right now, but some patterns indicate that accelerant was used inside and outside the trailer, as well as the vehicle," Harrison said. "I'll be in touch."

"Thanks." Reese watched as the man walked away, and it finally hit him: he had nothing left but the clothes on his back. His computer, and what few things he owned, had been burned to the ground. Gone. Up in smoke. Just like that. "I think I might need to head to Walmart to get some clothes and stuff."

"Why don't you come stay at my place?" Jared offered.

"Thanks. As much as I love your wife and kids," he said to Jared. "I think I'll take a hotel."

Jared nodded. "I best get home. See you first thing."

"A hotel is nuts. Stay with me. I've got an extra bedroom," Frank said.

"Not sure that's a good idea."

Frank shrugged. "I'm not sorry I hit you. I'm still insanely mad. But I can't change the situation, and if you're really buying The Heritage Inn, then I need to make sure you sure as shit don't ruin my view."

Reese let out a small laugh. It felt good. "I need to go get some things at the store first," Reese said.

"No worries," Frank said. "I'll wait up, but don't make it too late."

"All right."

Reese got in his truck, then headed north toward Ticonderoga and the local Walmart. He parked close to the front door, then mindlessly grabbed a shopping cart and headed in, his brain working on fumes. He picked up the basics. Toiletries, underwear, socks, T-shirts, a couple pairs of jeans, and a pair of sneakers. Enough to get by, for now. At the checkout, it struck him: he had no emotion. He was simply flat. Exhausted.

It took him about thirty-five minutes to drive down Route 9, following the lake until he got to Harmon Hill. The Harmons were an interesting lot, and it had taken time to get used to them. All of them, for the most part, had respected his desire to be private. No one pushed to find out too much about his past until he started dating Patty. Even then, probably because half of the Harmons were Marines, and the other half law enforcement, they seemed to understand.

Now? He could sense the difference in the family, and it made him sad.

He rolled the truck to a stop next to Patty's SUV, noticing that Patty's lights were on. They had texted a couple of times since the fire, but he didn't expect her to still be awake.

He closed his truck door and snagged the bags from the flatbed. He stood on the porch, starting a text to Frank, when the upstairs door opened.

"I'm so glad you're okay," Patty said. "I'm really sorry about the car. I know how much you've always wanted that Mustang."

"It's just a car."

"The images on the news looked pretty bad." She took a few steps down toward him. "Why don't you come up?"

"I feel like shit, and I just spent the last few hours at an unwanted campfire. Frank said I can crash at his place, but he didn't want me to be late. School night and all."

"I told him I'd cut you off at the pass, and I've got beer. Come on up," she said.

She placed a six-pack of beer on the top step. She took one out, cracked it open and held it out to him. "I know it's no consolation, but I did want to congratulate you on your offer being accepted for buying the hotel," she said. "I guess it's my attempt to look for the silver lining."

"Thanks." He made his way to the top of the stairs. He looked deep into her eyes. "I'm sorry you had to find out about my past the way you did. I'm heading to visit Nana in a week or so, and I want you to come."

"I don't know." She leaned against the doorjamb of her bedroom, her nightgown slightly see-through, which distracted him from everything, and maybe, just maybe, that was a good thing. "I don't think I'm ready to meet any of your family."

"I understand," he said. "Though I'm going to have to tell Nana about the baby, and it would be nice to have you there with me."

"I think I'll let you do that on your own."

"I really do want to make this work."

"I believe that you do," she said. "It's not that I don't, just that I'm scared."

He drained his beer, then cracked open a second one, realizing they had more to fear than all the changes in their lives. "I don't think the fire was an accident." He took her by the hand, leading her into the bedroom. He sat on the foot the bed, and she joined him. "I don't have a handle on what's really going on or why, but I'm worried, and I need to keep you and the baby safe. I'm going to see if I can rent the main house, and I want you to move in there with me."

She shook her head. "That house is too big. I'd be scared alone. Besides, there are more people here to watch out for me." She glided her fingers across his cheek. "I'm more worried about you, especially since the fire wasn't an accident."

"Then I'll stay here with you," he said softly. "I'm happy we're having a baby. I want him or her with everything I am." He pressed his lips to hers. She didn't pull away but didn't exactly participate.

She pressed her hand against his chest, finishing the kiss. "Just for tonight. I won't move into that house right now."

"I don't want you to be alone."

"You're never alone on Harmon Hill," she said. "I can't live with you right now. It's too soon. Like you said before, we start over."

"All right." He cupped her face, looking her in

square in the eye, and saw her confusion, sadness, and pain. All of which he alone had caused. "We both want this baby. We will be good parents together."

A single tear rolled down her cheek, and as he kissed it away, she wrapped her arms around him, burying her face in his neck, and began to sob. "I was so scared you'd been hurt in that fire."

Patty had spent a good hour pacing in Lacy's family room when the call finally came through that Reese was fine. Part of her was pissed as hell he hadn't called, texted, or whatever. The other part was just so damned grateful the father of her child was fine. Frank had given her the evil eye for telling him Reese would be staying with her for the night, but she had wanted to congratulate him on his purchase. It was a step in the right direction for them.

Mostly, she had to see him. Touch him. Feel him. She needed to know he was okay. Now, she found herself pressed against his hard body, drying her tears in his shirt. She grasped at his back, desperate to hold him tighter, unable to get rid of the thought that he could have been in that trailer when it went up in flames.

To his credit, he held her tenderly and whispered sweet, kind words as he stroked the back of her head and neck. He didn't tell her to stop, or that it would all be okay. He just held her and told her he was there, for whatever she needed. She had no idea what she needed. She knew in the bottom of her heart that he would be completely capable of putting his child first. She believed beyond any reasonable doubt that he would love and adore his child. It didn't matter that the child hadn't been planned. She saw that so deeply, it made her want to forget about anything and everything in the past. Even the things she didn't know. Life was a risk. Love a bigger risk. It was time to take the leap of faith and stop fighting what she couldn't change if she tried.

She loved Reese.

"I don't want to do this alone," she whispered. "I was so worried something bad had happened to you."

"You don't have to be alone in this, ever." He lifted her head off his shoulder, studying her intently.

"I don't think—"

He pressed his fingers against her lips. "Don't think. Just feel."

Oh, how she felt every single inch of him. And she had to admit, if only to herself, it wasn't just physical. It was love. His lips were hot on her neck, kissing every inch as they made their way to her lips, which she gave without any battle or trepidation. He pressed her back to the bed, gripped her hips, his knee gently parting her legs, and his chest heaved into hers with the force of passion.

She devoured what he offered. It wasn't about him or her anymore, but about the deep connection they shared, and one that needed to be strengthened. That connection might not have created the baby, but it was going to have to raise that baby, and if in a moment of compassion they needed entangled bodies, who was she to fight it?

They fumbled at each other's clothing. Thoughts of the future came crashing down, but instead of facing them, she straddled Reese and quickly slipped her nightshirt over her head, losing herself in the sensation of his hand caressing one breast and his tongue dancing across the other. She kissed her way down his chest, across his stomach, her fingers grappling with his belt.

"Slow down," he murmured.

"No."

Their lovemaking had never been slow, but wild and relentless. He flipped her onto her back, spreading her legs, easing his fingers inside her while his tongue and lips caressed her, bringing her to perfect climax. Her body quivered beneath his touch, and before it was over, he was fully inside her, their hips locked tightly.

"Don't stop." She coaxed him, slowly but firmly, needing more release. "I need you," she whispered.

He matched her motions, and she felt his own buildup rise, making it all the sweeter. He took his time, something he'd always done, but this was different. In the past, he'd simply made it last, a game of teasing that often brought her to multiple orgasms. But this time he was tender. Gentle.

He raised his body above hers, still grinding his hips, bringing her right to the edge, but never over the top. He kissed her nose, and she opened her eyes and gasped as she stared into his eyes, filled with something more than mere sexual excitement. She wrapped her legs around him, pulling him in quickly, and then ground her hips. His eyes rolled back as he let his own climax spill out into her. Watching him forced her release to hit the surface seconds later.

She embraced his full weight as he collapsed, his

breathing labored. They remained entangled in each other for a long time before he rolled off, still holding her close. Her last thought before she fell into a deep sleep was what it was going to be like to have this whenever she wanted or needed.

Chapter Nine

Normally, the smell of bacon in the morning would excite Patty, but now it only made her rush to the bathroom with a wave a nausea and a few dry heaves. She knew Reese was trying to be nice by making her breakfast, and she did appreciate it, but she couldn't handle the smell.

"You okay?" he asked.

"Morning sickness. I think."

"Oh, sorry," he said. "Can I get you something else?"

"Just crackers, please, and maybe some coffee. Oh, and crack open a window. I don't think I like bacon anymore."

"That's going to suck for a while." He pointed to a mug on the table. "Just a little cream."

"Thanks." Other than feeling sick, she wanted every morning to be like this. The two of them sharing breakfast and light conversation before they headed out the door for work. She paused, lifting the mug to her lips and blew, contemplating the job situation.

So much of her life was changing, and she believed it to be for the good. Only one tiny little complication. She hated harping on his marriage, but it was a fact. She knew he was trying to find his wife and divorce her, but so much of what was happening had been a direct result of an unplanned, but wanted, baby. It was hard not to wonder what would have happened between them, or not happened, if she hadn't gotten pregnant.

He put a roll of crackers and a glass of water on the table. She sat, sipping the perfectly brewed coffee while reading a few texts on her phone.

"What's got your attention?"

"Frank."

"What does he want?"

"He's just worried."

"About what?"

"Me. Us. The situation. Holland. Lots of things."

"I am, too," he said, and even without looking, she sensed him watching her. "Are you avoiding me?"

A loaded question, but right on the money. "Last night was... Well, it was... I was so scared that you really could have been hurt."

"You said that last night," Reese said. "What's really on your mind?"

"I can't get over the fact that you're still married. I'm worried you're still keeping things from me, and it makes me want to forget about last night."

"I'm not keeping secrets. If something concerns you, just ask."

"Okay. What's going on with finding your wife?"

"My PI guy says she went dark about a year ago, but he's checking her last known address and place of employment," Reese said.

"See, I didn't know that. So I wonder what else you don't tell me."

"I'm not keeping anything else from you. The big things are on the table. Anything else you want to know, all you have to do is ask. I'm going to prove to you—"

"You don't have to prove anything," she said. "I guess I feel out of the loop."

"I didn't think you'd want me reporting back

every detail about finding my soon-to-be ex-wife," he said. "I need to get to work. See you tonight?"

She nodded.

He kissed her gently on the lips, letting the kiss linger.

He let out a long sigh, resting his forehead against hers. "I'm not going anywhere and we'll get through this. Call me if you need me." She watched him go down the flight of stairs, where he was greeted by a very unhappy Frank, who glanced between the two of them.

"I'm not sure it's a good idea for you to be staying here," Frank said

"Not your business," Patty yelled from the top of the stairs.

Reese held out his hand. "I'm here to stay."

Frank took it and the two men shook. "You rip her heart out, I'll do more than hit you."

"I'm sure you won't be the only one in line for that." Reese turned and looked up at Patty one more time. His eyes filled so many emotions, except one. Fear. "Lock the doors."

She nodded, waved, then pulled her robe tighter. This was really happening.

Patty had no desire to leave the house, but she sucked it up and made herself presentable. She had to return some things to Conrad's office, since she was no longer employed, and pick up the severance package.

The spring air had finally started to stick. There was more brown grass than snow. The sun shone brightly in the sky, and while it was still only about fifty, that was spring in Lake George.

The drive down Route 9 was filled with pleasant thoughts, until she pulled into the parking lot of the law offices of Conrad Winston. The first thing she noted was the fancy schmancy car. The second thing she noticed was Jared across the street at the coffee shop. He was leaning against a patrol car, sipping coffee, looking quite menacing. The man did look like a legend in the making.

Then Frank stepped out of the coffee shop. He and Jared made eye contact, but did nothing to acknowledge each other's presence. Why were they there?

She grabbed the box of stuff that belonged to Conrad's law office, then opened the front door, using her back to push it open.

"File whatever injunction you need to. File them

all. Bury him in paperwork. Do whatever you can think of to stop that sale."

Patty didn't need to turn around to know that silky-sweet voice with the bitter edge belonged to Keith Holland.

"Oh, hi, Patty," Conrad said. "Thanks for returning all the files promptly."

"Not a problem."

"I haven't given up on buying The Heritage Inn." Keith glided into her personal space. He was smooth and charming and intimidating, all at the same time. And those eyes. It had to be how deep and blue they were. She tried to avoid them, but it was impossible. "I want it for my family. I think you, of all people, can understand that."

"Excuse me?"

"Harmon Hill," Keith said. "It's beautiful, and all owned by your family. I want that for my family. You know, I have five grandchildren now. Five." He shook his head. "I want to make sure my family—the ones that have stuck by me—are well taken care of."

"I'm sure you'll find the perfect place," she said. "Conrad, may I have the paperwork on my severance package?"

"I had Angela put it in the mail," Conrad said. "I

am sorry things didn't work out. I will give you a glowing reference if you need it."

"Thanks," she said, but she noticed Holland's expression of glaring disdain. "I appreciate it." Without waiting for any fanfare, she walked out the door. For the last year, she'd given this job her best. Her termination felt like a manipulation of billing hours, but she could do nothing about it.

She got into her car, noting that Frank and Jared were still across the street. Still leaning against the car. Still sipping coffee. Whatever they were doing, they certainly weren't trying to be secretive.

That scared her. She texted Reese, asking what the heck was up with that. He responded that he'd talk to her tonight about it, and he asked if she wouldn't mind setting up his things in the main house since he was renting until he closed on the property. He also told her that a patrol car would be going by The Heritage Inn and Harmon Hill, just to be safe.

The idea he was taking such precautions made her jittery. She called Lacy, hoping they'd be able to help move Reese into the main house together. She did not want to be alone.

Chapter Ten

The morning had been overwhelming for Reese. They'd hit brick wall after brick wall when it came to figuring out who was responsible for the fire, as well as connecting the dots to Terry, Conrad, and Holland. Stacey had hit a dead end with the law firm. Mary wouldn't give her a thing, and without a warrant, she didn't have to.

It was three in the afternoon, and the sun was still high in the sky, warming the chilly waters. A pounding headache had been looming all day. Reese had been hoping for a couple more nights with Patty. He'd begged her to come stay with him. She met him with a resounding no. He continued to flip through the paperwork on the fire that had destroyed the trailer and his Mustang, while managing a few more begging texts.

"You look deep in thought," Jared said, standing over him with a deep scowl, like a father with his son. He and Frank had just come in from patrol, but had yet to brief him on anything.

"I'm contemplating."

"About what?" Jared asked, sitting down.

"First, who really has motive to burn up my trailer and car? Because saying it was Holland makes sense on the surface. You and Frank saw him at Conrad's, where Patty mentioned some weird shit about him still wanting the place for his family." He looked at his boss, who still had that fatherly look that drove Reese nuts. The man wasn't that much older. "Why do you always look at me like I'm twelve, or something?"

Jared shrugged. According to his wife, he did it to everyone, even people much older. "So, what do you think?"

"Even if Holland wanted me gone that badly, a Mustang and a trailer aren't going to scare me off the sale, unless he somehow hinted it was him. That it would get worse if I didn't back off. He's done no such thing, and so far, while all sorts of rumors about him being 'connected' run rampant, we can't find anything that says this guy would even think about doing that, much less hire someone."

"All right," Jared said. "Who is out and about, and who has the biggest grudge against you?"

"It's not a very long list. Hell, Frank has more enemies than me."

"Well, make the list, right down to a kid you punched on the playground in the second grade."

"Already on it."

The front door pushed open, and Stacey breezed in. "Let's hit the road!" She didn't bother taking off her standard-issue coat.

It was the first time Reese had seen her show up in full uniform. "I guess fifty-two degrees means no more Eskimo parka?"

"You're a funny guy," she said. "So, we ready to roll?"

"Good Lord, girl. Relax," Jared said. "You're just going to be sitting in a car for hours."

"Yes, sir," Stacey said.

"And don't call me sir." Jared shook his head. "You know I hate that."

Reese laughed. He'd gotten used to this group of people, and he suddenly felt a sense of belonging that he hadn't felt in a very long time.

"Anything to report before we head out?" Reese asked.

"Holland's still at the Edgar Resort, last we checked. Conrad is still at court, according to our sources. Nothing much going on, so basically, normal patrol," Jared said.

"Well, that's no fun," Stacey said.

"You can get another job, if you like." Jared lowered his head and gave Stacey the evil eye.

"You know," Stacey said, "I've brought in a lot of intel. I think you need to cop to the diaper thing."

"You haven't connected it all," Jared said. "Do that, and we've got a diaper deal."

"Do we always have to talk about Stacey's diaper and bony ass?" Reese asked.

"Get to work, the both of you." Jared turned, laughing as he disappeared into his office.

"Heard the fire wasn't an accident." Stacey put a cylindrical box on the desk.

"How did you know? I just found out."

"I know people."

"Of course you do."

She pushed the cylinder closer to him.

"What's that?"

"The final blueprints for The Heritage Inn. Doug

said he filed them this morning. You'll only need three variances to complete phase one."

"Can your dad get me a list of things to ask the owner about now?"

"I'm sure he can."

Reese opened the cylinder, then slid out the papers. The blueprints were held together by a rubber band that also secured an envelope. He pulled it out, then read the handwritten note thanking him for giving them the project and assuring him they wouldn't let him down.

"Seriously? How much money do you have?" Stacey asked.

Not a question he was used to being asked, much less answering. "Enough that I'm not going to tell you. Ever."

"That's fair," she said. "Is that the report of the fire? Can I see it?"

"Yep," he said and handed it to her.

She flipped open the file then started reading. He watched as she turned the pages, made a few faces, then folded it shut and leaned back. "What does Jared think?"

"He wants names of the people I put behind bars, or who might see me as an enemy."

"I put my money on Holland."

"Why do you say that?"

"Funny you should ask that." She pulled out a piece of paper from her purse. "I got this from someone I know who works with Mary in the Albany office. Seems it was Holland who paid the legal fees for Terry."

"Well, that sort of sheds new light, now doesn't it." He grabbed his phone, texting Patty one more time. While looking into other suspects was due diligence, he knew in his gut Holland was a dangerous man.

Stacey nodded. "Let me give this to Jared before we head out."

He waited, grabbing his coat and his Stetson.

"It's so weird to know you're rich," she said.

"I get the impression your dad is pretty well off." Reese grabbed the mini-computer. "Let's go, bony-assed little girl."

She smiled coyly. "On your six, boss."

"Don't ever call me boss."

"On your six, bossman."

He laughed, but immediately turned his expression stone-cold when she went for the driver's seat of the patrol car. "Listen, rookie," he said. "I'm driving. Period. Got it, bony-assed little girl?"

"Should I let my father know you've been checking out my ass?"

"Should I let your boyfriend know you check out Doug's ass every chance you get?"

"That is so not true." Her cheeks turned five shades of red, so Reese knew he was on point, but decided it was best not to harass her anymore about it, or her total denial. Something he could relate to, since for months he'd been in denial about how he really felt about Patty.

The next half hour or so was silent. They parked in one of the No U-Turn positions on the Northway. Reese held the radar gun while Stacey searched the portable computer and took notes. She'd been pulling Reese's arrest records and also digging into his background, per Jared's request. Reese knew she was doing it. He also understood why. He was too close to the problem himself, and often by profiling the victim of a crime, you came across the perp. "Maybe we should go after that guy," Reese said, putting the radar gun down. "Clocked him at—"

"Well, that sucks," Stacey said as she shoved her cell phone in front of his face. "Dad says there have been four different injunctions filed against the sale of the Heritage."

Reese read the texts. "Patty said she overheard

them talking about that at the office, but said it was bullshit."

"It is," Stacey said, "but effective to stall a sale."

"So, essentially—" Reese's thoughts were cut off by Jared barking over the radio.

"Locals were called, but I thought you might like to know Patty called in a 9-1-1. Seems someone broke into her house while she was gone. She's fine, so don't freak out."

"On my way," he said. "Buckle up, little girl."

"Drive faster, old man."

He grinned. You needed a dry sense of humor in this job. "I'm going to like working with you."

"Jury is still out on if I'm going to like working with you," Stacey said. "We really need to work on your driving skills and teach you a thing or two about sarcasm."

Chapter Eleven

Patty knew, the moment she went for her keys while juggling two bags of groceries, that the front door was ajar. At first, she thought Andy had forgotten to secure it again, but he hadn't done that in months. After she kicked the door closed and looked up the stairs, she knew something wasn't right. The door to her apartment was wide-open.

She stood there for half a minute before deciding she'd rather have the cops come than risk someone being up there, ready to point a gun at her. Again.

She got in her car, turned it on, locked the doors, then called 9-1-1 and waited, ready to drive away the moment an intruder came out the door.

She was grateful when the local sheriff showed

up within six minutes. The officer walked her through the apartment. Nothing was taken, but Patty noticed, with shock, a floral arrangement nearly identical to the first one Keith Holland had sent. This one had no card; instead, it had a dead rat right in the middle of it.

The officer had the audacity to ask if the building had a rat infestation and wondered whether the plant was poisonous. Patty felt a surge of rage knot in the pit of her stomach and was about to let the officer have it when a furry creature scurried across the kitchen floor. Then she heard the noises in the walls.

Rat issue aside, that plant wasn't there when she'd left this morning; her door had been open, and someone had been in her house. She placed both hands over her belly.

Reese and Stacey showed up while the officer was still there. Reese made her feel safe. Secure. She knew she should have called him directly, but he probably would have told her to call 9-1-1 first, then call him. By the look of annoyance on his face, she realized she'd done what she'd been accusing him of doing: leaving her out of the loop.

Patty wrapped a blanket around herself while Reese talked with the officer. Stacey walked through her apartment, and then Frank's. Frank, his wife, and Andy were away at a school function, so Patty let Stacey in.

It was hard not to stare at Reese. When they first got together, she couldn't believe a man that looked like Reese would want to date a plain Jane like herself. She wasn't sexy like Lacy or demure like Ryan, but Reese always made her feel beautiful. And, she thought as he glanced her way, he made her feel important.

"I'm going to call my dad," Stacey said.

"Why?"

"To have him get one of his rodent buddies to check if this is really a problem that's been here for a bit, or something else because if you'd had this problem you'd know it, so I gather it's the former."

"Thanks," Patty said, understanding Reese's frustration and amusement with the young trooper and her massive use of words and the speed at which they left her mouth. "I was beginning to feel crazy."

"You're not crazy, but we'll need to get those rodents exterminated before you can move back in."

"Frank is going to be pissed about that," Patty said.

"It won't take long, especially if what I suspect is true."

"And what's that?"

"Someone brought the rats in. And," Stacey continued, "I think they cut a fresh hole in the back of the house, let them in through the walls, then tried to patch it. Did a shit job of that, too."

"Why would someone do that?"

Stacey shrugged. "We also need to find out where those flowers came from. You said the first one was delivered?"

Patty nodded.

"Do you have any of the packaging? The plastic wrap? Where is the card? Do you remember who delivered them?"

"Geez, you really are the Energizer bunny."

Stacey didn't laugh. "Seriously. We need all this."

"I don't know. I threw it all away, including the plant, but the card was signed Keith." Patty focused on Reese and the officer. It didn't look like the conversation was pleasant, but they shook hands, and the officer got in his car and drove away just as a shiny black truck and a beat-up pickup pulled in next to Reese's patrol car.

"Wonderful," Stacey said. "He brought the bitch."

"Huh?"

"Sorry," Stacey said. "Very unprofessional of me." She pointed to the handsome man getting out of the shiny truck. "That's Doug, my father's business partner. In the pickup, his wife. We don't like each other."

"Ah," Patty said. "Mary Nesbitch. She has the quite the reputation."

"You know her?"

"I'm a paralegal. I've met her. She's one tough nut. Highly driven and motivated." Patty wanted to add that Mary was the kind of career-minded woman that gave women a bad rap in general.

"I can't stand her."

Stacey's anger was palpable, so as Doug and Reese came toward them, Patty was glad Mary stayed in the truck, phone to her ear.

"What did the local say?" Stacey asked as Reese approached.

"Basically said to call an exterminator," Reese said. "What did you find?"

"Well, I think the rat situation was planted," Stacey said.

"How so?" Doug asked. He was much cuter up close and personal, but he had that deep distance in his dark eyes that Reese used to have in his blue eyes.

"Be easier if I just showed you and the rodent expert my findings."

Patty couldn't believe all that had transpired in the last few days. She felt dizzy and leaned into Reese.

"You okay?" Reese asked.

She shook her head. "I've been shot. Held at gunpoint. Lost my job. Pregnant. And now some wacko is putting rats in my apartment. How would you be?"

"Pretty shitty."

Patty welcomed Reese's dry sense of humor at a moment like this. She'd spilled enough tears over the last few days. "What's going on here? Because I'm going to fall apart at any minute. None of this makes any sense."

"I wish I had a real answer," Reese admitted. "I wish I didn't think it was all connected. You being held at gunpoint. The weird threats from that Holland fellow. The fire. The rats. Four separate injunctions filed against my offer for the hotel by Holland. All roads lead back to that asshole."

She shivered. "You really think it's all connected. Some crazy plot? But why?"

"I don't know." Reese's voice grew dark. "We need to take steps to make sure you're safe."

"You're scaring me."

"I'd be lying if I said I wasn't scared," Reese said.

"But I'm going to put an end to all this bullshit. I promise you. Stacey, Frank, everyone at the station is working on this. I've got Jim looking into the injunctions, but I'm going to need a good lawyer. What are your thoughts on Doug's wife?"

Patty shook her head. "She's ruthless and probably good at her job, but I wouldn't hire her. She gives me a bad vibe." Everybody right now gave Patty a bad vibe.

"She and Doug make an odd couple," Reese said.

"I don't think they're happy."

"I think Stacey has the hots for Doug." Thankfully, Reese's tone had leveled off, doing what he did best, redirecting.

This time, however, she was glad for the deflection, easing her rising panic. "Your best bet would be a land lawyer who understands contract law, and the best one I know is Andrew Taft of Taft and Associates."

"Actually, I believe that's who Jim uses," Reese said. "I want you to stay with me tonight."

He'd eased closer and looped his arm around her, pulling her close against his strong frame. She felt safe there. Before she could answer, Stacey and Doug made their way around to the front of the house.

"What's the verdict?" Reese said.

"I can't be a hundred percent positive, but a piece of siding was cut off, and the wood behind it was also cut out, then nailed back in. Looks recent. It would be easy to put a small animal between the walls and trap them there. My guy says he can take care of the problem, but everyone will have to vacate for forty-eight hours."

"Not a problem," Reese said. "I'm renting the main house at the Heritage, so we'll all stay there, but it's a crime scene now, so I can't have him doing that until we have a few other things taken care of."

"I've called in forensics, so they will dust for prints," Stacey said.

"On a more positive note, one of the injunctions has already been tossed," Doug said. "I suspect another will be by the end of the week. The one that will give us trouble is that Holland Development is claiming they had a verbal agreement with Chris Riley, one of the owner's daughters, before Reese's offer came in and LuAnn Riley accepted it."

"They countered the offer and gave me until end of the day to accept. I accepted immediately, and the paperwork has been signed. What's the issue?"

"Holland is saying that LuAnn had no idea of a verbal offer and acceptance by the other sister. Until that offer is accepted or rejected, the sale can't go through."

"That sounds nuts," Reese said. "What do I do?"

"My wife is an attorney. I can ask her—"

"I suggested Andrew Taft," Patty said. "He specializes in things like this."

"I think he'd be better than Mary," Stacey said. "I know Mary has been working fourteen-hour days, and her boss has her jumping through hoops to make partner, so why add more to her plate?" It was obvious Stacey added the latter just to keep the peace. "Besides, Taft is the lawyer you use for all your land and contract deals."

Maybe it wasn't to keep the peace, but to poke Doug. Patty wondered if these two had any idea the sparks that flew between them. She leaned into Reese.

"Let's go!" Mary yelled. "I've got to get back to the office."

"Guess your dinner plans just got canceled," Stacey said.

"At least I had dinner plans," Doug said. "Didn't Todd the Toad make up some excuse not to come see you this weekend?" Doug turned his attention back to Reese. "Contact Taft. Tell him we sent you. I'll fax him over all the information we have."

"Thanks for your help."

"No problem." Doug turned and headed toward his truck.

"I can see why you like his ass. It's pretty sexy," Reese said.

"What?" Patty looked at Doug's ass, which, she had to admit, was nice, but was totally confused by Reese's comment.

"You've been hanging around Jared too long," Stacey said. "And by the way, Patty, your boyfriend has been looking at my ass. Says it's bony."

Patty buried her face in Reese's neck and started laughing. The entire conversation was absurd, but oddly, made total sense. More importantly, it eased her fear.

"Well, let's get your bony ass back in the patrol car. We're not off duty." Reese tossed her the keys. "And you're not driving. I just need a moment."

"Men," Stacey muttered.

"She's interesting," Patty said.

"She's going to be a good cop, once we duct tape her mouth closed." Reese rested his hands on Patty's shoulders. "I want you to gather a few things and go right to the main house." He pressed the keys into her hands. "You'll be safe with me. I'm off at midnight. I'll let Frank know what's going on, and

I'm going to ask him, Lacy, and Andy to stay, too. There's plenty of room."

"I bought sheets for the two beds that are there. But really, there's almost no furniture."

"It will be enough for now. Don't worry, we'll get to the bottom of this and end it."

"I'm just tired of feeling on edge." She considered staying with a relative, or a friend, or even at a real hotel, but she didn't have the energy to fight him. Or her own desires.

"I know," he said. "I'm sorry for my part in all of that."

She allowed him a quick kiss on the lips before letting him go. "Don't waste any time," he said. "And text me when you're at the house. I'll be sending a patrol car to check in on you. Don't hesitate to call 9-1-1, and then me." He arched a brow.

"I won't hesitate," she promised.

Chapter Twelve

Patty felt comfortable in the residency, even though it was scantily furnished, and the fact she was alone. Reese texted her every thirty minutes. Frank called every hour and even Stacey had gotten in on the action.

The family room had one sofa and a coffee table with a lamp. The living room, dining room, and den were all empty. The master bedroom had a bed and a single dresser. The bedroom at the end of the hall had the same, while Frank had brought a cot for Andy. She'd gone up to bed the same time Lacy, Frank, and Andy had, around ten, but she couldn't sleep until she heard Reese come home. She'd been so bone-tired, she fell fast asleep as soon as she'd confirmed it was indeed Reese. She slept through the night, though she had a mixture of good and bad dreams. When she rolled over, she expected Reese to be by her side.

He wasn't.

Panic rushed through her body as she bolted out of the room and down the stairs. She stopped at the entrance of the family room. Reese was sleeping on the sofa, his one leg bent, his knee peeking out from under the small blanket and one arm behind his head.

"Morning," Reese said, breaking her from her thoughts. He rolled to the side, stretching as the blanket dropped to the floor. "Sleep okay?"

"I did, thanks," she said, staring at him in his boxers as if it were the first time she'd seen him nearly naked. "You could have slept upstairs. It's a big bed." She couldn't hide the disappointment she felt in the tone of her voice.

"I didn't want to wake you," he said. "When I went upstairs, you were so sound asleep, well, I figured you needed it."

"I did." But she needed him more, a thought she kept to herself.

"Is the morning sickness bad?"

"So far, it's just bacon that sets it off. I was just about to go make some coffee. Want some?"

"That would be great."

She paused at the picture window, taking in the beautiful view of the lake. The sun was rising from behind the house, casting a glow across the water. A few fishing boats hummed along the shoreline, a sure sign that spring was on the way.

"Nice view, huh?" Reese asked.

"One of the best," she said. "Want some breakfast to go with that coffee?"

"I'll just make some frozen waffles. I bought some on my way home, which reminds me, I bought some of those breakfast bars you like so much."

"Thanks."

She pushed through the swinging kitchen doors, which Patty had always thought weird. If she owned this place, the first thing she'd do was get rid of the doors and tear down some of the walls, opening the kitchen up to the family room. But it wasn't her place.

But it could be, she thought with a quick beat of her heart. Her place with Reese. Things had changed so much between them, and she had started to trust him again. Trust that he'd tell her anything she asked. Trust that he wasn't keeping some other deep, dark secret. Mostly, she trusted that what was going on between them was real. It would take time. There were no guarantees.

But the possibility made her smile.

The kitchen had little in the way of food and utensils, but she managed a full pot of coffee. She was pouring two cups when the doorbell rang. She froze, not wanting to see who could possibly be at the door at eight in the morning, much less at a house that the world had no idea was currently occupied.

Reese burst through the kitchen doors. "Shit," he said as he opened the door in his boxers. "Nana, what the hell are you doing here?"

"Didn't you get my text?" a scolding female voice said.

"Two seconds ago."

"I sent it yesterday," a woman said. "And you're the one telling me to check the phone more often."

Patty turned, surprised to see a woman in perhaps her early seventies, with the most beautiful white hair she'd ever seen, standing in the doorway. She had the same facial features as Reese, and she was tall, with a figure to die for.

"You could have called. When did you get here? Why are you here?"

"You wanting to buy a hotel is a big change. Too

big. I came to see what is really going on with you," she said. "I have to say it was hard to find you. Nice of you to tell me the rental you were living in had burned to the ground." There was no mistaking the resentment and hurt in the woman's voice.

Patty watched, still stunned, as this woman kissed Reese on the cheek and then pushed her way into the kitchen.

"Hello," the woman said. "And you are...?"

"Nana, this is Patty. Patty, this is Elizabeth Baxter, my nana."

"Nice to meet you," Patty said.

"You, as well," Elizabeth said. "May I ask what kind of a relationship you have with my grandson?"

"Nana," Reese said. "You're out of line. And I'm not twelve."

"Perhaps," Nana said. "You've got a lot of explaining to do, young man. Get me some coffee, and then start by telling me why you've chosen to keep certain things from me. Like the trailer, and why you want the hotel—and no offense Patty, but what does she have to do with this?"

"I didn't want you to worry, so I chose not to tell you about the fire." He glanced at Patty, who just arched a brow, seeing it finally sink in for him how the smallest of things, even done out of love and kindness, could be misconstrued as secretive and uncaring. "I want to buy this hotel and this house because I like it here. I want to live here. And Patty and I... we're going to have a baby."

Nana gasped and covered her mouth with both her hands. "I feel like I just went back in time."

"It's not like that," Reese said.

Patty knew this was going to be one hell of a breakfast. "Can I make you some eggs?" she asked, unable to think of anything else to say to diffuse the tension.

"I'd love some eggs," Nana said. "And bacon. You've got bacon, right?"

"No bacon," he said. "It makes Patty nauseous, so just eggs and toast. Or frozen waffles."

"I'll take eggs and toast," Nana said. "Now go put on some clothes, and then we'll talk."

"Yes, ma'am."

Patty was mortified. The last few days had been a blaze of insanity, and she had not a single thing to say to this woman. So, as she cracked open a few eggs and put some toast in the toaster, she continued to say nothing.

Elizabeth Baxter took off her coat, put her purse on a chair, then sat down.

"Cream? Sugar?" Patty asked, placing a cup of

coffee on the table but turning instantly to the pan, sizzling with a bit of butter.

"Black, please," Elizabeth said. "How far along are you?"

"Almost three months," Patty admitted. She felt a wave of nausea, which could have been discomfort, or just morning sickness. She figured it was a combination.

"What stake do you have in Reese buying this property?"

"None," Patty said, turning to face Elizabeth. "This is Reese's idea. His place. His deal. I want nothing from Reese. Nothing." Which wasn't entirely the truth, so she added, "He wants to be a part of the baby's life, so that is all I want from him."

"What do you know about his past?"

"Enough to know—"

"Nana, this is none of your business," Reese said as he finished pulling a shirt over his head.

"You are too full of secrets," Elizabeth said. "Why didn't you tell me about the baby, or this young woman?"

"Because I wanted to tell you in person," he said.

Reese sat at the table next to Elizabeth, placing his hand over hers. "When did you get here?"

"Yesterday evening. This morning, I went to the address I had, but it was a burned-down trailer. Why on earth were you living in a trailer?"

"Please tell me where you stayed last night," Reese said. He had an uncanny ability to redirect people, and Patty suspected he got that from Elizabeth.

"The Village Inn," she said. "Then I met this lovely woman named Stacey when I went to the station house first thing, and she told me about you staying here with this young woman as if I knew everything about your life. Quite the little talker, that one."

"One of these days, it's going to get her in trouble," Reese muttered.

Patty placed a plate of food in front of Elizabeth, then a couple of waffles and syrup in front of Reese. "Can I get you anything else?"

"No, thank you," Elizabeth said, then took a few small bites of toast. "I don't know how to feel about all this. It feels so complicated. Rushed. I know you're a grown man, but really, do you understand my concern?" she asked.

"Of course I do," he said. "The only complication is Jessica. Otherwise, Patty and I will work things out."

Patty wanted to agree with Reese, but she found herself tongue-tied.

"I have to find and divorce Jessica," Reese said.

"Then what?" Elizabeth asked. "No offense. I'm sure you're lovely"—Elizabeth pointed to Patty—"but if you know about Jessica, you know my grandson hasn't had the best judgment when—"

"That's enough," Reese said. "I know you're upset, but that's no way to treat Patty. She's a good woman. With a good heart. And she's the mother of your great-grandchild, so a little respect, please." Patty wanted to wring his neck for speaking to his nana that way, but his defense of her made her flush with warmth.

"Oh, Patty," Nana said. "I do apologize. I'm taking my anger out on you when I should be putting Reese over my knee. I had no right to say those things. Please understand, I'm just a little shocked."

"Should have seen the look on my face when I found out Reese was married."

Elizabeth cracked a smile. "Can we start over?"

"Of course we can," Patty said. "I'll leave you two alone to catch up. I need to go get dressed." Though for what, she had no idea.

"You should have told me you were coming," Reese said, shifting the food around on his plate, knowing he was playing with fire, but the silence after Patty left the room was deafening. Nana had a way of being able to sit quietly in a confrontational situation, waiting for someone, anyone, to break the ice. It was almost never her.

"You've got some nerve," Nana said. "Seems your secrets go way deeper than an 'oh by the way, I'm coming to town.'"

"You're right." Reese shoved the plate away. "I am sorry you had to find out about the baby... about...everything this way." When he'd been nine, he lied to his grandparents about breaking a vase. He'd tried to glue it together. Thought he'd done a damn good job, until Nana asked him to get it and put some flowers in it that she'd just received from the governor's wife. Nana explained to him that one always filled the vase first, then cut the stems, then put the flowers in the vase. She told him to go give it a try, then bring the arrangement back into the living room where she'd been entertaining eight very important and powerful guests.

He should have learned his lesson then. Nana knew everything. If she didn't, she'd find out.

"You should be more than just sorry." Nana moved gracefully about the kitchen, putting dishes in the dishwasher, then refilling her cup. She'd been wealthy her entire life. Old money. So old, no one really knew where it had come from. The daughter of a philanthropist and married to one of the richest men in the state, but they always lived a relatively unflashy lifestyle. Where their friends had a couple of estates in various cities or countries, half a dozen cars, and at least two private jets, and made sure the world saw their fancy toys, the Baxters usually chose to fly commercial. They drove what Reese always considered normal cars, and Reese didn't even know his grandparents were rich until he was in his late teens.

"I really did want to tell you in person, but I have some things to work out with Patty."

"Such as...?"

"Everything," Reese admitted. "I had no idea how much I cared for her until she dumped me, then a few weeks later, she told me she was pregnant. It's been a bit of a roller coaster ride since then."

"Just because you get a girl pregnant, doesn't

mean the first thing you do is run off and get married—"

"I can't marry Patty until I'm divorced, but that would be the plan, eventually."

"Being honorable is not always the best thing. I thought you would have learned that the first time."

"I agree," he said. "This time, it's not about honor. It's what I want. I've dug a hole just deep enough with Patty that I've got a lot of making up to do. But we are getting through it."

"You really care about her?"

He nodded. "I have a lot of changes to make. A lot of wrongs to right, and a lot of proving to do."

"Actions, my dear boy."

"I know." His first action of the day was to deal with the injunctions. As long as Chris Riley signed the affidavit that stated there was no binding verbal agreement, then he was golden. He had a meeting with Andrew Taft right before work, so that should get the ball rolling on that end. He was going to have to get Patty to work closely with Andrew on all the legal stuff. He knew the law pretty well, but he didn't know lawyering.

"You find out anything about Jessica from her family?" Reese asked.

Nana reached for her bag, a large one, usually

filled with everything but the kitchen sink. She rummaged around in it for half a minute before pulling out a small envelope. "My contacts didn't find out any more than your PI friend. Seems she's disappeared, but here is everything up until then, and she's nothing but a con artist. Her family has disowned her, and her mother looked so sad just talking to me about it that I felt bad for her."

"I appreciate you asking them," he said. "The money for the down payment on this place? The financial reports?"

"In my briefcase in the car," she said. "But until you are divorced from that gold-digging, baby-murdering hussy, or we find out she's dead, this hotel will be in my name. Do I make myself clear?"

"Yes, ma'am."

"Now, I suppose there is another bedroom for me here."

"I have two other houseguests. It's a long story, but we'll need to buy some furniture for one of the other guest rooms."

"Perhaps I will take Patty with me."

"I don't think that's a good—"

"I don't care what you think." Nana looked at her Apple Watch. "I was told you need to be at work soon, so you should go clean yourself up. Tell Patty

I'll be back in an hour with my things, and she and I will spend the day shopping."

"I don't think she'll—"

"Just stop thinking," Nana said. "It's too painful."

Reese heard giggles coming from the other room. He hugged and kissed his nana and then watched her walk out the door. He stood in the kitchen, waiting to be harassed by Frank, Lacy, and Patty.

It was starting out to be a banner day.

Chapter Thirteen

Patty had been looking forward to spending the day with Reese's nana, but she needed to address the injunctions and meet with a lawyer on Reese's behalf. His nana seemed genuinely grateful that Reese had Patty to take care of those things. Patty didn't know how she felt about anything, other than that meeting with Andrew meant a possible job opportunity, and she wasn't going to feel guilty about taking that opportunity.

His offices were in Bolton Landing, a small town off the east shore of Lake George. He rented space over a diner on the corner of Main Street. There was a small reception area and two offices, one for him and one for his partner. The furniture was a dark cherry. The reception area had a brown leather sofa with two matching wingback leather chairs. Both rooms had built-in floor-to-ceiling bookshelves lined with legal books and journals.

"Everything looks good," Andrew said. "I'm making copies for Reese, but we should be able to push this sale through in a couple of days, as long as we get the affidavit signed by both Riley girls and a judge, stating there was no previous verbal offer with Holland Development."

"We're working on that," Patty said. "Thanks for your help on this."

"My pleasure. I have a couple other projects I would like to contract you to work on. I can't give you full-time hours, or even an office, but I can pay you for your time."

"I'm good with contract work." Andrew was short, in his early fifties, with a thick head of graying brown hair. He was fit for his age, and while he didn't look old, he didn't look young, either. Nothing about the man stood out, except that he was genuinely a nice guy.

That went a long way.

"I'll let you know when I get that signed affidavit," Andrew said.

Patty decided to go out on a limb. "Have you ever worked with Holland Development before?"

"No," he said, "but I have friends who aren't fond of him or his development company."

"Why is that?"

"Holland doesn't fight fair." He handed her a large envelope. "That's everything you need to stop that one injunction. Once I get that signed affidavit, I'll push everything through, and Reese should be rid of Holland for good."

"Thanks. We really appreciate it." Patty took the envelope, then made her way to where she'd parked on Main Street, constantly looking around, feeling as though someone could be watching. Her heart beat a little faster. She quickly texted Reese, letting him know her whereabouts. Normally, that would be silly, but right now, it felt like she was being smart. The sun was bright, the snow nearly gone. If she had reservations about Reese, they were quickly melting like the snow. Deep down, she wanted him to have this hotel, and she wanted him to be part of her life.

No. She wanted to be with him. Simple as that.

Her phone rang. She quickly got in her car and put it through Bluetooth, then pulled out on the street, heading toward Route 9. "Hey, Lacy," she said. "What's up?"

"Talk to Reese or Frank in the last hour?"

"No, why?"

"The sheriff's office determined the rat infestation was intentional. I guess they were able to identify the rats and where they came from."

"That's creepy."

"More than creepy, and it gets weirder," Lacy said. "They came from a medical research facility that reported a break-in yesterday, and over fifty rats went missing. The same rats that showed up in the house."

"Who would do that?" Patty pulled onto Route 9, looking forward to navigating the twists and turns without the snow and ice. She took the corners tight, but not too fast. She slowed as she approached the intersection, tapping gently on the brakes.

"Everyone thinks it was Holland," Lacy said.

A loud bang ripped through the car as it jolted to the right. "Oh, my God!"

"What's going on?" Lacy asked, but Patty didn't have time to answer, much less figure out what had happened or what to do next, because the world went black.

"What do you remember?" Reese knew he sounded more like a cop than a concerned boyfriend, but he was in uniform, in the hospital, taking a statement from the victim of a potential crime.

"I got in the car. I was talking with Lacy, then I heard a loud bang, and then I don't remember anything until I woke up while the EMTs were pulling me from my car."

Reese checked his phone. Still nothing from Stacey, who was currently looking into what caused the tire to blow out.

"How old are the tires?"

"Less than a year." Patty had adjusted the hospital bed to a sitting position. Her legs were slightly bent, two pillows tucked beneath her back, one under her knees. Reese had heard about the accident over the radio. He'd been on patrol when Lacy called 9-1-1, and Jared had forwarded the information to him. As he raced to the hospital, fifteen minutes after Patty, he realized that while he wanted the baby to be unharmed, he wanted Patty to be okay even more. He wanted the woman he loved to be all right. If she were good, he could survive anything.

Now they were awaiting her OB/GYN. Patty had been given a clean bill of health, but they had yet to confirm the health of the baby.

"Rotate them regularly? Check the pressure?"

"Three months ago. Not lately."

Reese poked his head out of the curtain, hoping to expedite the needed tests, but it didn't seem to be working. "Did you see anything suspicious?" He checked his Apple Watch for any information from Frank, Stacey, or Jared. So far, nothing.

"I'm really scared." She rested one hand over her stomach, rubbing gently.

He sat on the edge of the bed. "There have been too many strange things going on for me not to be concerned that this wasn't just an accident."

"I should be scared, then."

"I really don't want to frighten you," he said. "But I'd be avoiding the truth by omission if I said otherwise."

"Thanks for being honest." She smiled faintly, still rubbing her stomach.

"Have you felt any movement yet?" He placed his hand tentatively over hers. "You've never told me when the baby is due."

"You never asked." She smiled at him. "Based on my last period, around November twenty-first, but they said a sonogram will be able to give us a more accurate date."

"So, you've been to the doctor?"

"Just for a blood test. Not to see the doctor." She shook her head. "My first appointment is next week. You can come. Actually, I'd like it if you did."

"Just tell me when, and I'll be there. Do you think we'll be able to hear the heartbeat?"

"I think we'll be able to hear it today," a woman's voice said. Reese looked up to see a woman no older than him, wearing scrubs.

"Hey, Doctor Noonan." Patty laced her fingers through Reese's, squeezing tightly.

"How are you feeling?" The doctor stood on the opposite side of the bed, glancing at Patty, then flipping through pages in the patient chart.

Reese wasn't sure if he should continue to sit or stand. Introduce himself? Leave? Ask questions? Before he could finish contemplating his next move, Patty tapped his shoulder.

"Reese, you okay?"

"Um, yeah, why?"

"Because I've introduced you to my doctor twice, and you've been sitting there, staring at nothing, saying nothing."

"Oh," he said. "Reese McGinn. Nice to meet you."

"Likewise," Dr. Noonan said. "So, as I started to

tell Patty, I'm going to check the baby's heartbeat using this device." She held something in her hand. "Normally, we can hear the heartbeat at about ten weeks, and Patty is right about the eleven- to twelve-week mark, if our calculations are correct."

"What if you don't hear anything?" Reese asked.

"Let's not worry about that right now," the doctor said. "Dad, do you mind moving for a moment?"

Reese looked around the room, half expecting to see Patty's father. "Oh, you mean me."

Dr. Noonan smiled. "You might as well get used to the title."

Reese hadn't even thought about being called 'Dad.' He was still getting used to the idea that he was going to *be* one, not actually have someone, anyone, call him by that name. When he rose, Patty didn't let go of his hand, so he stood at her side, giving her support. Or maybe she was giving him support. His heart beat so fast and hard, he figured it could be heard a mile away without any listening device.

"I'm going to put some gel on your belly. It might be a little cold."

Reese watched the doctor squeeze the gel, then

rub it around with a little handheld thing, and the device picked up a thumping sound. A very loud and strong thumping sound. It mimicked what he felt in his chest, but was even faster.

"Baby sounds good," Dr. Noonan said.

"What a relief." Patty looked up at Reese, her eyes moist with tears, but her smile so big and so happy. "Reese?"

"Yeah," he managed.

"You're hurting my hand," Patty said.

"Oh." He quickly let go. "That was…that was…"

"Your baby," Dr. Noonan said. "I think all is well, but since I like to err on the side of caution, I'm going to order a sonogram before I let you go today. It shouldn't take long. They won't be able to say anything to you, but I'll be back to discharge you and will fill you in on the results."

"Should we be worried?" Reese asked.

"I'm sure all is fine, but you were in a car accident, so I think it's best we take a look," Dr. Noonan said. "Perhaps Dad might need to sit down, and we should get him some water."

Reese heard all the words. They registered in his brain. But for the life of him, the room wouldn't stop swaying. His vision blurred, and he couldn't utter a single word, so he let the doctor lead him to a chair, and he sipped the water she handed him. He had no idea how long he sat there. He suspected only a minute or so, but it felt like hours. "I'm fine," he said.

"Are you sure?" Patty asked. "You look a little pale."

"I'm fine," he said with more authority as he pulled himself out of the shock of being called Dad. Since hearing the word, then his child's heartbeat, a rush of emotions had flooded his brain, a combination of his past and his present colliding. Something that never had a chance, and the sadness that tore through his heart for so many years slowly gave way to the promise of a future he once thought he could never have.

"That was pretty cool." He stood, adjusting his belt, then placed his hands on his hips in the best manly and authoritative-cop stance he could muster.

Patty smiled again. "Reese McGinn," she said. "You're starting to be a bit of a sap."

"Funny girl." He moved back to her bedside to give her a wet, sloppy kiss, but his cell phone rang.

"I've got to take this," he said. "It's Stacey."

Patty nodded.

Reese stepped into the hallway just as he heard

the doctor tell Patty that hospital transport would be by shortly to take her to the sonogram.

"What did you find out?" Reese asked, skipping the formalities.

"Bullet hole," Stacey said.

"Got the bullet?" Reese asked.

"Sent on to ballistics, but I suspect it was from a military-grade sniper rifle."

"That doesn't make sense. Why Patty? Why now? The only person giving us any trouble is Holland."

"I know," Stacey admitted. "But Frank found an eyewitness who says they saw something where Patty's tire blew. Figured you'd want to be there for questioning."

"I'm leaving now." He hated to leave, but her safety depended on him finding out why someone would want to hurt her. That was his job, both as a trooper and as the man who loved her.

Reese stood at the door of the master bedroom, where Patty was most likely sound asleep. The house was quiet. His grandmother was tucked away in her new suite. Frank, Lacy, and Andy had returned to

Harmon Hill. Reese's hand trembled as he gripped the door handle. There had been an emotional shift between him and Patty, but he wasn't quite sure what it meant for her. He knew what it meant for him.

The connection he felt to her was far more than having a child. Life without Patty would be no life at all. He prayed to a God he never believed in that she felt the same way.

He wanted to feel it was wrong of him to sneak into her room, but it felt right. More than right... It felt natural. Normal. She'd also mentioned it was a big bed. His heart had been with her for a long time. It just took his brain a while to catch on. Running from it because he'd gotten burned had once seemed like a great way to protect himself, but it had only made him lonely. And he'd been a very lonely man for the last seven years.

Not anymore.

Patty had the curtains open, and the moon cast a gleam across the bed and the polished hardwood floor. The only other pieces of furniture were a dresser and a small nightstand, but he could picture a big sleigh bed. Maybe dark cherry. Matching dressers, bed tables, vanity. A small bassinet for the baby. Maybe even a dog at the edge of the bed. A big, cuddly golden retriever. It was almost too much to dream for.

Patty lay on her side, her back to him, hugging a pillow. He slipped out of his uniform, then put his gun in the top drawer of the dresser. He left his shirt and pants on the floor, then tucked himself under the sheets, pulling her close.

"I was hoping you'd visit me tonight."

He twitched, her voice startling him. "I want you to be safe."

"I have mixed feelings about you."

"I'm not surprised," he said.

"I feel safe with you, though." She pulled his arm tighter around her midsection.

"How are you holding up?"

"Okay." She rolled over and faced him, slipping her knee between his legs. "Want to see a picture of the baby?"

"You have one?"

"Doctor Noonan brought it to me once the sonogram checked out."

"I'm sorry I couldn't stay."

"I understand." She sat up and turned on the lamp next to the bed and handed him a picture. "See that?"

"Yeah."

"Baby," she said. "Doing just fine. The doctor adjusted the due date to November nineteenth, but all is well in babyland."

"We're having a baby." The words still sounded surreal rolling off his lips. With everything going on, he hadn't really allowed himself to embrace it. Now, he never wanted to let it go.

"Why is this happening to us?" She looked up at him with big doe-like eyes. "Why does someone always want to hurt me? First, the whole thing last year with Lacy and being at the wrong place at the wrong time. And then Terry. The rats. And I know the tire was hit with a bullet."

"I wish I had an answer." He reached around her to put the picture back on the nightstand, switched off the lights, and settled back under the sheets. They lay facing each other, gazing into each other's eyes. It wasn't sexual. Or even romantic.

Just comfortable.

"I know it's Holland, but I can't prove it. Yet."

"So, why me?" Patty had tucked both her hands up under her cheek.

"It's not you," Reese said. "I think it's both of us. He wants The Heritage Inn and he thinks we're blocking him from getting it. All I want is to keep you safe." He ran his fingers up and down her arm, enjoying her soft skin. Everything about her was perfect. "We'll find a way to nail Holland."

"Maybe it's not him. Maybe it's your wife."

His breath hitched. Bringing up Jessica was like putting a knife through his heart. "Doubtful. She's not smart enough to pull something like this off on her own. She's a two-bit con-artist," he said. "From what Nana and the PI gathered on Jessica, she worked one con after the next. Her parents disowned her. That says a lot."

"It's also kind of sad."

"I have a hard time feeling sorry for her," Reese said. "Brad, my PI, is talking with her last known employer and has a lead on her last roommate and some guy she swindled for a couple grand a few months ago."

Patty let out a long sigh. "I'm sorry. I can handle everything else but the marriage thing. Actually, it's not so much the marriage, but the kind of woman you married."

"I—"

She pressed her finger against his lips. "You didn't know. I get that. But until you're divorced, it's hard for us to move forward."

"We'll get there. I promise." He kissed her nose.

"I want so much to say things to you, but I don't want them to be just words, at just any moment."

"I feel the same," she said. "Let's just get some sleep. We both need it."

He tucked his own hands under his head and closed his eyes, but sleep didn't come. All he could think about was that he lay in bed with the woman he loved, and he was pretty sure she felt the same way.

He blinked a few more times, then noticed she was staring at him. "What?"

"Nothing."

He smiled. "You want me."

"You're impossible."

"But adorable."

"Yes, you are," she said. "Tell me something I don't know about you."

"I'm really scared."

"About what?" she asked.

He reached for her, and she let him wrap his arms around her and rested her head on his chest. "Honestly, everything. All the bad things going on. The baby. Mostly about how much I have hurt you."

"I forgive you."

"I do love you, Patty. Baby or no baby. I love you,

and I want to show you in a million different ways," he said. "It might have taken a baby to open my heart, but I loved you long before I knew I loved you."

"You can be very romantic and sweet," she said. "I want to believe you. I want to tell you how I feel, but I know we wouldn't be in this bed together had I not gotten pregnant. I think you can understand my trepidation."

"Of course I understand it." He also understood her words didn't match her body's reaction to him as he gently caressed her exposed skin. She inched closer, their legs intertwined as she ran her fingers through his chest hair, an intimate act that only lovers shared. "I wish I hadn't walked away when you broke up with me. I was hurt and shocked, but what was I to say? You were as much a part of our so-called deal as I was."

"You could have said you didn't want to break up."

"And would you have listened? Would you have wanted to give us a chance?"

"I don't know. You never asked," she said. "That's key. You gave up."

"Well then, so did you."

"I guess I can't argue that."

He pressed his thumb under her chin and tilted

her head, looking directly into her beautiful eyes. Eyes he wanted to get lost in forever. "I love you," he said. "I know you think I'm being honorable and just doing it because of the baby. I admit, the baby made me realize how I really felt, but the truth is, if I had left here, I would have been even more lonely and lost than I was when I got here. Worse, because when I moved here, I didn't know I was lonely, but leaving you... Well, there wouldn't be much to live for after that."

"I do believe you," she said. "I feel so cared for by you, but you have always been so distant, it's hard to trust that this new emotional, loving Reese is going to last."

"This is the real me," he said before ravishing her mouth, not giving her the chance to deny him anything. She could stop him. No doubt about that. He'd get out of that bed and walk away if that was what she really wanted.

Her body, however, screamed for him. Her tongue dove deep into his mouth, matching his passion as she pulled him closer. Her legs wrapped so tightly around him that if it weren't love, she'd have strangled him. She stroked his arms, thighs, ass, every inch of him. She was desperate for him, and he for her. But he couldn't allow himself to give all of himself unless she admitted how she really felt.

He pushed her a few inches away. "Say it."

"No."

"Say it," he demanded. "I love you, and I know you feel the same way, but I need you to say it."

She struggled with her clothing, doing her best to rip it off her body, as well as remove his boxers. It was impossible to resist. He stopped pushing her away and suckled her breast, teasing her with his fingers. They stared at each other, their breathing labored, their bodies covered in sweat that glowed under the moonlight.

"Say it."

"I don't want to." She placed his hand over her breast, pushing her nipple between his fingers.

He squeezed, then released. "I love you." He rolled on top of her. "Tell me," he demanded. "And mean it."

"Oh, for crying out loud," she said. "I love you, okay? Now can we please just get to the good stuff?"

"Say it and mean it," he said softly.

When she looked deep into his eyes, he didn't really need the words. His heart raced with anticipation. He felt her love. His world would be complete.

"I love you," she whispered.

His body shuddered as he let out a small groan, dipping his forehead to hers. "I love you back." He entered her slowly. He locked gazes with her, and he wasn't going to let her turn away or close her eyes. She would see with every stroke of his body, with every sensation he could give her that she was safe with him, and always and forever, he'd belong to her.

He was in love for the very first time in his life.

Patty perched herself on the new oversized recliner Nana bought for the living room and watched the first of the sun's rays appear across the bright-blue waters of Lake George.

"Comfortable?" Nana's voice rang out from behind Patty.

"Very much, thank you."

"Did you sleep well?" Nana stood in front of the large picture window facing the water.

"I did." Patty blushed. Being in Reese's arms, feeling every part of his love without any reservation had helped lull her into a deep sleep where wild dreams of their life together gently glided across her mind. She could see it so clearly. It felt so right and so good, she had no desire to wake up.

"No cramping? Headache? Anything at all from the accident?" Nana asked, her voice full of concern.

"I'm feeling good," Patty assured her.

"Can I get you something?"

"Tea would be nice."

"Let me cook you a good breakfast," Nana said.

"Anything but bacon." Patty followed her into the kitchen. Nana had been trying so hard after their first encounter, and they really seemed to get along. That was good.

Patty sat at the table, looking out the window toward The Heritage Inn. The tree cutters were hard at work now that the injunctions had been settled and the sale finalized. Reese, Doug, and Jim were at the inn going over some of the plans. It should have been a happy time all around. She believed every word Reese had said last night, and his lovemaking was like nothing they had ever shared. They should be enjoying their future.

But an overwhelming sense of doom loomed over her, making every breath difficult. Reese was still married, and someone was doing their best to cause them bodily harm, or at the very least, scare the heck out of them. It was working.

Nana looked up, pouring coffee into a large thermos. "They will catch whoever did this."

"I just hope it's before someone gets really hurt." Patty's fear was all consuming, and she didn't like it one bit. She was used to being in control, but in the last year, her life had spun far off the track. She knew what the next step should be, but so many other factors blocked it, and it made her head spin.

"Why don't you take this to Reese and the construction guys. What are their names? They seem like nice men."

"Doug and Jim and they are decent and kind." Patty took the thermos and did as instructed. It surprised her how warm the air felt when she stepped outside, but it didn't do anything to make her feel better, and the moment she hit the parking lot, away from the dense trees behind the house or the welcoming water of the lake, she felt exposed. In danger. Fearful. She quickened her pace across the pathway to the inn.

"Ma'am," yelled some guy with a chainsaw. "This tree is coming down. Please make sure you stay away from this area." He pointed to a large patch of grass on the opposite side of the residency, down near the lake.

She nodded, then met Reese at the door to the inn.

"You okay?" he asked.

"No," she admitted. "Nana thought you might like a fresh pot."

"Thanks," he said. "I don't want you to worry. We've got a good team, and we're working with other law enforcement. We're going to figure this out," he said as if he could read her thoughts. That idea, under normal circumstances, should have warmed her to her core. The man she loved, taking care of something that threatened their very existence.

But it only reminded her of all the obstacles, even after he got full ownership of the hotel. "What if it's not Holland?"

"I'm good at my job and I trust my instincts. It's Holland."

"Excuse me," Doug said. "I left my laptop in the truck. Back in a sec."

"Go back to the residency," Reese said. "I'll be over in a few."

Patty followed Doug out the door but passed his truck as she headed for the residency, making sure she stayed clear of where the tree was to come down.

Something crackled in the background as the noise of the chainsaw stopped. Patty turned to witness a tree snapping in half. Only it didn't land where the man said it would. Instead, it crashed down on top of the black truck in the parking lot, leveling it to the ground.

The black truck that Doug Tanner had just gotten into.

Reese stared at the smashed truck, wondering how the hell Doug had escaped with nothing but a couple of scratches.

"You're one lucky man," Reese said.

"I heard the tree snap, looked up, and just hauled ass."

"That tree was supposed to go in the other direction," Patty said, standing next to Nana, who had raced out the moment Patty let out a bloodcurdling scream. "At least, the tree guy said so."

"Glad they were insured," Doug said. "Damn, I just got that new car smell out of that truck."

"Then we'll buy you a used one," Jim said. "The damage to the porch is minimal, so I'm hoping that's all that was done to the structure of the inn. We'll have to check the foundation."

"I don't mean to scare you two," Reese said. "But I don't think that was an accident."

"Trees snap the wrong way all the time," Jim said. "We've seen it before."

"There have been too many strange things going on for me to believe this was a simple accident. My trailer—burned down. Patty's house—infested with rats. Her tire—shot with a rifle. Now this? I'm not normally the conspiracy kind of guy, but this is just too much." He nodded toward Stacey. "By the way she's talking to those two workers and the local, she's thinking the same thing."

"Huh," Jim said. "She actually looks like she knows what she's doing."

"She's the best rookie I've ever worked with," Reese said. "Since you've worked with this tree company before, tell me about those two over there."

"I've never met them," Jim said.

"Neither have I," Doug added. "It's a big company with a large turnover and lots of seasonal workers, so we don't know everyone. Come to think of it, there was no warning before the tree came down," Doug said. "Normally, no matter the direction, someone yells a warning, and if it's going in the wrong direction, they'd say."

"That's true," Jim said. "I've been near trees going the wrong way, and it's quick, but people tend to make noise when it happens, especially if it looks like it's landing on someone."

"Anything else out the ordinary?" Reese asked. "I wasn't paying attention." Doug walked to the tree and examined it more closely. "The chainsaw marks are on both sides of the tree, which isn't unusual, but heavier on the side toward the parking lot. It's cut wrong."

Reese assessed the situation. The locals were talking with the tree guys and Stacey, who gave him an odd look. No, it was one of those coded-message looks, and he understood she was sending him a message about how full of shit and absolutely scared the tree guys were. *So, that's how that works,* he thought.

"Nana," Reese said, "why don't you and Patty go back to the house?"

"It's called the residency," Patty corrected him.

"Fine," Reese said. "The residency."

"You go," Nana said. "I'll be right along." Nana leaned closer to Reese and whispered in his ear. "Patty walked across that driveway seconds before the tree fell. She and Doug came out, then the tree came down."

"I know," he said, struggling to think logically

and not let his personal attachment to Patty affect his ability to do his job.

Nana scurried off to catch up with a very shaken Patty, while Reese made his way to Stacey and the local cops.

"Doug," Stacey yelled. "We need you to go to the sheriff's office and make an official statement. I'll drive you. Dad, you need to go, too."

"What?" one of the tree guys said. "It was an accident."

"We understand," Stacey said. "We need you to go as well. All standard procedure. Nothing to worry about, and best for the insurance."

Reese was impressed by the way she worked the tree guys.

"Does it have to be done now?" the other tree guy asked.

"Best if it's done now," Stacey said. "Get it out of the way." Stacey nodded to Reese, and he knew she would follow the crew to the local office and get statements and whatever else she could, because she didn't believe this was an accident any more than he did.

It was nice to be able to be in on the super-secret glances and actually understand them.

Reese made his way back to the residency. He

entered though the back door into the kitchen, making sure to take his muddy shoes off. Patty and Nana were at the table. Patty didn't even look up, just sat there pushing her food around on the plate.

"I don't get it," Patty said.

"Get what?" Reese sat next to her, taking the plate Nana pushed in front of him. He was going to be in for one hell of a long day.

Before Patty could answer, a fancy, loaded SUV pulled down the private driveway. Not the parking lot, but the residency's private access road. Reese clenched his fists as he saw Keith Holland and two of his cronies get out of the vehicle. "Why don't you two go to the other room?" He stood, opening the back door, not paying any attention to Nana standing right behind him. "I think it best if you leave," he called to Holland.

"Now, now. Let's be civil." Holland held his hands up. "I'm here to talk. Work things out."

"I'm not backing out of this deal."

"Well, hello there, Elizabeth. Long time no see."

Reese looked from Nana to Holland. The idea that their paths had crossed before made his stomach turn.

"He's the other guy who tried to buy this property?" Nana asked. "You didn't tell me it was Holland Development. Keith Holland."

"You know him?" Reese looked from an angry Nana, something he didn't see often, back to a very amused Holland, something that terrified him.

Holland smiled wide. "Boy, you look a lot like your mother, you know that?"

"How do you know anything about my mother?" Reese asked.

"Elizabeth didn't tell you? Tsk, tsk."

Reese glanced over his shoulder. Nana was as white as a ghost. "Tell me what?"

"Maybe after she tells her story, with whatever spin she chooses to put on it, you might change your mind about backing out of this deal," Holland said.

"That's not going to happen." Reese clenched his fists.

"We'll see," Holland said. "I want this for my family. My true family. The one that has stuck by me. Not bribed me or tossed me away like garbage. You get that, don't you, son?"

"I have no idea what you are talking about," Reese said.

"Sure, you do." Holland laughed as he eased back toward his SUV. "Your mother abandoned you like you meant nothing. Wonder what your father did? Why he did it? Ask your nana about that."

Reese watched Holland and his crew drive away.

"Nana?" Reese closed the door and stared his grandmother down. "What the hell is he talking about? What does he know of my mother and my father? Is he talking about Allen, or my biological father?"

"I think we all need to sit down," Nana said.

Reese didn't like the sound of that.

Chapter Fourteen

"How do you know Holland?" Reese yelled as he rattled the floorboards, pacing in front of the kitchen table. "Better yet, how does he know my mother? Or anything about my father?"

"Patty, would you excuse us?" Nana asked.

"No," Reese said. "I've excluded her from the truth for far too long. She stays." He turned to Patty. "I want no more secrets between us. Please stay."

Patty nodded and continued to stir her tea. She didn't look happy, but at least she didn't run off.

Progress.

"I'm waiting." Reese wasn't in any mood to try to piece this shitstorm together. Nana was holding out on precious information that could protect Patty and his baby. He was going to get that information if it damn near killed him.

"Sit down, Reese," Nana said. "I hate it when you pace like that."

"I think I'm fine standing." If he didn't keep moving he might go crazy. "No amount of deflecting is going to get you out of this one. So, let's start with how you know Holland."

Nana sat across from Patty, palming her coffee mug, while Reese paced a path by the back door. He'd always known there were things Nana didn't share. Things about his mother, all in the name of protecting him. He thought he'd uncovered most of them, like his mother selling herself for drugs. Like the idea that his father was just some young, irresponsible kid. Hell, his mother had only been seventeen when he'd come into this world. He accepted the lies by omission, because dealing with his mother had been a living hell and he didn't need to know more about her crazy life. She'd done enough damage. He was sad she died. But he wasn't sad she'd left him to be raised by his grandparents.

But this didn't feel like a truth hidden to protect him. This just felt like a lie. He understood now why Patty had been so upset.

"Holland was the contractor for your grandfather's new building. The one that is currently corporate headquarters."

"When was that built?"

"Your mother was about fifteen when it started. Holland Development was just getting started, but Keith Holland was a brilliant architect, and your grandfather took a shine to him. It was too late before we put everything together. Grandpa was devastated. Took him years to get over, though I'm not sure he ever really did."

Reese had already put together more than he wanted to, the clues so obvious it was impossible to deny. "Holland didn't finish that project, did he?"

"No," she said. "A year into it, we realized your mother and Holland had been sleeping together. Your grandfather paid Holland quite a large sum of money to go away."

"You're saying he bankrolled Holland's current empire?"

"Essentially, yes. Your grandpa wasn't proud of it, but he blackmailed Holland to leave you and your mother alone."

"Blackmailed him how?"

"Threatened to have him arrested. For statutory rape."

"Jesus," Patty said. "You let him get away with it?"

Nana shook her head. "Eleanor, Reese's mother, thought she was so in love with Holland that she would have run off with him. She tried."

"What stopped her?" Reese asked.

"Holland hit her a few times. Told her to go home to Daddy. That she wasn't ready. Of course, Holland was already married to another woman. Eleanor was so naïve, she thought Holland would leave his wife."

"Did he know she was pregnant?" Reese closed his eyes. He had no memories of his mother from before age two or three, but a few good ones lingered in the recesses of his mind. Playing at a playground. Her reading to him. He couldn't remember if and when she'd changed, but the rest of his memories were of him putting her to bed. Cleaning up her vomit. Making her breakfast. And sometimes, being left alone for days.

He did the same for Allen. He remembered periods when Allen was clean, but not many. Those four short years, until Reese turned seven and moved in permanently with his grandparents, were still etched so deep into his psyche that there was no erasing them.

"Not then," Nana said. "When we found out, Grandpa went to Holland and paid him off, holding that over his head, since they had proof of statutory rape."

Reese had seen his grandfather as invincible. This seemed so out character for him to blackmail anyone. Grandpa had always held people accountable.

"Reese was that proof," Patty said.

"That is pretty fucked up," Reese said. "Mom just went along with this?"

Nana nodded. "She wanted you so badly. We worried she was going to try to get back with Holland. And she did. She took you to the city, to his posh new office. You were about a year old."

"He met me?"

Nana lowered her head in shame. "I don't know what happened there that day, other than Eleanor came home, packed up her things, and told us to go to hell. Later, we found out he wouldn't even see her, and sent someone who worked for him down to tell her if she ever contacted him again, he'd destroy Grandpa. He told her we paid him off. She found out what a monster he was that day. But she also believed we were no better. She took you, and we didn't see you for an entire year, until she came begging for money. We, of course, gave it to her, to take care of you. She'd been seeing Allen. He was a decent enough fellow."

"This is insane." Reese plopped himself in the chair next to Patty, who took his hand.

"Allen was the first guy she met after she moved out with you. We tried to get her to leave you with us. But she was eighteen. You were her son. We helped her as best we could. Helped Allen get a decent job, but he was into drugs, and so was your mother."

"I visited Allen in prison after Mom died. He told me he was sorry, but that was about it."

"He and your mom were meth addicts," Nana said. "Grandpa told them he'd take care of them if they went to rehab and got straight. That didn't last long. Then Allen was arrested for murder."

"So you made that go away. Made me think that the man I called dad just up and left me."

Nana nodded. "We thought, your mother included, that it would be better for you to believe that than to hear the truth. Your grandfather and I talked your mother into moving in with us and for a while, she stayed sober. But she took off a month later, leaving you with us and eventually giving us custody until she was diagnosed with cancer. She waited too long to seek medical treatment, and it was too late. Stage four, inoperable and incurable." Nana dabbed her eyes. "She was my little girl and no matter what, I loved her with all my heart."

Reese knew that to be fact, but it didn't change a fucking thing. "So, my real father is Keith Holland, who is somehow connected to some pretty bad people, who are now, for whatever reason that I can't even fathom, either trying to kill the woman I love, or scare us enough to run and hide. Do you happen to know why?"

Patty gripped his hand, and for the first time in a long while, he realized he had someone in his corner, no matter what. He squeezed tighter. He was never letting go.

"No," Nana said. "For a while, when you were little, we kept tabs on him, but then we realized he was off doing his own thing. He had a family. A wife and kids, and had long forgotten about the young girl he'd knocked up. We were glad to be rid of him. Allen was the lesser of two evils, or so we thought at the time."

"Allen was sent away for murder, a fact that shocked me when I found out," Reese said.

"He was a meth addict." Nana snagged another

tissue that Patty offered. "Outside of that, when he was straight, he was decent. Really, he was."

"He was a shitty father."

"Your mother wasn't going to get Mother of the Year, either," Nana said. "We just wanted to protect you."

"This is fucking unbelievable," Reese said. "You've known all along who my father was, and when I went searching for him, you discouraged me. Did it cost you a lot of money to derail my efforts?"

Nana rubbed her temples. "I wanted to protect you."

"All you did was encourage a life of lies, betrayal, and distance from people," Patty said.

"How dare you? I didn't do that; Jessica did," Nana said.

"No," Patty said. "How dare *you*? You should have told Reese the truth. You should have let his mother—"

"Once Keith refused to see her, and their baby," Nana interrupted. "She begged us to make sure Reese never knew. When she and Allen first got together, we didn't know he did drugs, or that Eleanor was doing them."

"And what about after you found out?" Patty asked.

"We thought we were doing the right thing when we paid for rehab many times, for both of them. He got straight a few times because of Reese, and he was always good to that boy. He married her, and if he could have stayed off drugs, he'd have been a good father. I know that with everything I am."

"What about my birth certificate? It clearly states that Allen is my father."

"We thought that best."

"Of course you did." Reese slammed his fist on the table and then stormed out of the room. If he didn't get some space, he'd say something he'd regret.

Patty followed Reese upstairs to the master bedroom. He'd slammed that door shut as well. She didn't bother knocking. He had every right to be mad as hell. Probably a whole lot of hurt and confusion. She knew exactly how that felt.

But they weren't the ones putting each other in such pain and anguish. It would be so easy for him to push all that down, stuffing it so deep in his soul that he'd never be able to connect to a single person again. She wasn't going to let him do that. Not now.

Not ever.

"Hey," she said stepping through the doorway.

He stood in front of the picture window overlooking the lake, his hands on his hips, his back to her, not turning and he didn't say a word.

"You can't change what they did," she said.

"I know." His voice was steady, but his tone bitter. "I think, deep down, I've always known Nana knew who my father was, but I was too scared to find out, so I never tried that hard. Then Jessica, and the baby happened. I thought I'd be able to stop the madness. All I did was make it a legacy."

"Not true." She wrapped her arms around his waist, clasping her hands up by his chest where she could feel his heart beating. She rested her head on his shoulder. "And even if it were true, you still have the power to change it with our baby."

He let out a long sigh. "I don't want to screw this kid up."

"You won't."

"I wish I believed that," Reese said. "I have to wonder why my mother would tell me...make me question who my father was...on her death bed. What was the point?"

"People do weird things when they're dying."

"I guess that's one answer I'll never know." He

raised her hands, then kissed them. "I'm a little shocked you haven't run to Harmon Hill as fast as possible to get away from the shitstorm that is my family."

"The thought has crossed my mind. But as you've been saying to me, I'm in this for the long haul."

"I've got to deal with this Holland thing."

Patty knew that to be the absolute truth, and it was more than just business. Now, it was personal. "I think I really need to rest. It's been a fucked-up couple of days."

"That's being polite," he said. "I brought in the mail." He tossed a few things on the bed.

She kicked off her shoes, then puffed up some pillows before settling in. "Great," she said. "Anything from Conrad? He said he sent over the severance deal, which means a check, and I have bills to pay."

Reese plopped down on the bed next to her and stared at the ceiling. "I'm sorry."

"For what?"

"Not telling you about being married. I should have done that long before the baby ever came around."

"I hate to admit it, but I understand why you didn't

tell me, but that was then, this is now. We know what secrets do to people." Most of the mail was junk, but an envelope from her former employer was at the bottom, much thicker than she expected for a last paycheck. She fiddled with the edges. "Just promise me that you will be honest with me going forward."

"I can do that," he said. "Jesus. Holland has known all along I'm his son, and he's been doing this shit to me. To us. He spouts shit about his family and wanting a place for them, yet technically, I'm family."

"Sperm doesn't make one a father, or family." She opened the envelope, then pulled out a folder. On top was a note from Conrad that read, *I'm sorry to do this to you, but please help me.* Patty flipped open the file, then started reading. It took a few minutes for the information to register.

"None of this makes any sense. Maybe that's why I didn't push too hard when it came to my biological father. I think I was afraid he didn't want me. I guess it just seems like Holland is going to a lot of trouble when it comes to the hotel and—"

"Reese?"

"Do you think he just wants to make me go away, or bring me into the fold?"

"Reese." She continued to scan the papers, ignoring his rant until one piece of paper stood out.

"You think this is all crazy, don't you?"

"Reese!"

"What?"

"I think I just found your smoking gun."

Chapter Fifteen

Reese white-knuckled it to the station. He wished he had a patrol car, so he could use the sirens to go flying around everyone. Now, he just looked like an asshole driver, but he didn't care. Jared had already left for the day, but said he'd head back to help with this situation. Frank and Stacey had been holding down the fort, and a couple of the regional guys were on patrol.

The truck tires squealed as he turned into the parking lot. He wasted no time gathering everything Conrad had sent over and racing into the station house. "Big room," he said, but everyone was already there ahead of him.

"So what, exactly, does Holland have on Conrad?" Stacey had rearranged the information on the boards in line with the few things Reese had told her over the phone.

"A few things." Reese spread out the paperwork on the conference table. "A couple of dicey pictures of him with women other than his wife."

"Everyone knows that about him," Frank said. "He thinks he's discreet, but he's not. And I don't think his wife cares."

"That's what Patty said." Reese figured that had been Holland's first attempt at blackmailing Conrad, and it didn't work. "But look at this." He pinned a letter up on the corkboard indicating that not only had Conrad never finished his law degree, but he never even took the bar.

"How is that even possible?" Stacey asked.

"I've learned a lot of the impossible can be possible these days," Reese said.

"That's very interesting." Jared took down the letter and read it again. "What else?"

Reese handed over a bunch of other paperwork regarding Conrad and school. "Graduating class list, and he's not on it. He managed to forge his law license."

"Who did all this for him?" Jared asked.

"That, we don't know," Reese admitted. "But I suspect someone associated with Holland. A few years ago, Holland approached Conrad to go over some accounting on a construction site. Said he needed an outside firm." Once again, Reese was pinning things up, and Jared was taking them down, then passing them to Frank and Stacey. Reese gave up and handed everything over to Jared. "Conrad found nothing wrong. Holland pushed him to find something wrong. Hence, Terry was fired for stealing money from the company."

"Okay," Jared said. "But can we backtrack a little more? Do we know why Terry had some high-priced attorney to get him out of his troubles?"

"A little fuzzy on that, but in the note to Patty from Conrad, he explains that Terry was some kind of muscle for Holland. Holland got pissed that Terry got caught more than once and wanted to get rid of him."

"Makes perfect sense," Stacey said. "But that doesn't explain Holland's infatuation with the Heritage or put any blame on him for Patty's rats, tires, or the trees coming down on Doug's truck."

"That's where it gets really weird." Reese straddled a chair and took in one very long, calming breath. "Open the file. Conrad had been doing some of his own digging into Holland, trying to find a way out from under him, and it turns out he was able to connect Holland back to my grandfather."

"Now, that is interesting," Stacey said as she tried unsuccessfully to yank the files from Jared. "What's the connection?"

"Holland was the developer for my grandfather's office building, but Holland didn't finish it."

Jared passed the file on. "That's all it says. But something tells me there is more."

"A lot more," Reese said. "Conrad hit a dead end because, like my grandfather, Holland is very smart, and they both made sure their little under-the-table deal was under lock and key. The only other person who really knew the details was my nana."

"She filled you in?" Jared asked.

"The short version is, Holland was messing around with my mother; she was underage, and my grandfather paid him off to go away and Holland did just that, especially because if he didn't, he would have gone to jail for statutory rape and my grandparents had the proof in the form of a child."

"Holland is your—"

"Frank," Reese said. "Don't say it, okay?"

The room went silent for a long moment as everyone digested that piece of information, along with everything else.

"Where's the smoking gun?"

"Conrad put a signed statement and a confession for his part in framing Terry in the paperwork he sent to Patty. He also kept track of everything illegal or near-illegal that Holland was asking him to do regarding the purchase of the casino site and The Heritage Inn. I sent a copy to the Feds. Just waiting for a warrant. Feds said they'd let one of us go with them."

"What's the charge?" Frank asked.

"A shitload of things," Reese said.

"Okay, but what I don't get is, why go after you if you're kin?" Jared said. "I think he'd want you to be in the fold. Part of the empire?"

"One would think," Reese said. "But my PI friend says Holland wanted to wash his hands of the whole thing because his wife and family think I'm just a bastard who doesn't deserve their respect or their money, and they see my purchase of The Heritage Inn as a slap in the face. I'm a bastard who is in the way of what he wants."

"Why didn't Conrad just come to us?" Stacey asked.

"Holland said he'd kill his family and make it look like Conrad did it," Reese said. "I believe

Holland could have easily done that, considering everything that has happened to Patty."

"That is one nasty motherfucker." Frank tossed a few pieces of paper on the table.

The pun wasn't lost on Reese, though he doubted it was intentional. "We will be able to nail his ass for what Conrad has, but we'll never get him for the trailer or the rats."

"Can you live with that?" Jared asked.

"I have to live with the knowledge that he was—is…fuck. Yeah. I can live with it as long as that asshole is in jail."

"You must think I'm a horrible person," Nana said.

"Not horrible," Patty said. "Misguided, perhaps." She didn't like being so abrupt with Reese's nana, but the lies were going to end now. No way would she bring a child into this world, in this situation, if honesty wasn't going to be the path to happiness. "Is there anything else Reese doesn't know?"

"I've told you both everything."

"Had all this been out from the get-go, we wouldn't even be having this conversation because Reese wouldn't have been so closed off."

"That's where you are wrong," Nana said. "You didn't know him before Jessica. That woman tore his heart out, and he never recovered. He never allowed himself to, until you."

"You don't think, if he'd known the truth of his heritage, that he would have been able to handle himself differently when it came to Jessica? I was not only unplanned, but I was unwanted." Patty held up her hand to shush Nana. "My mother didn't want me at all. She let my father, who did want me, talk her into a loveless marriage. It lasted years, but it screwed me up. Reese reacted so negatively to the abortion because Jessica never gave him the choice, and he wondered, after his mother died, if his mother had ever given his real father a choice. The genetics don't matter. It just matters to Reese that there was no discussion. In either situation…" Patty paused for a moment to collect her thoughts. "If Reese had known about Holland, well…"

Patty let the words hang. It was a cruel statement, and she shouldn't have gone that far with a woman she barely knew. She was about to apologize when she found herself staring down the wrong end of a gun.

Again.

"How long does it take to arrest an asshole?" Reese paced in the station house.

"Relax," Jared said. "That file will put Holland behind bars for years. We got the tree guys to roll over on him. We've got Conrad's information. Stop worrying."

"I won't feel better until he's locked up," Reese said.

"I have to ask," Jared said. "Doesn't it wig you out, just a little, that this man is your biological father?"

"Not really," Reese said. "Actions make you a father, and after a closer look at the facts, I realize that man knew all along that I existed. He saw me at Conrad's office. He knew when I pulled the trigger on Terry that I was his kid. He knew when I put in an offer on The Heritage Inn that I was his long-lost son, and he couldn't have that. To him, I'm a bastard, and my family was just a revenue source. A way to build his empire. He chose to take the money, build his company, make millions, and then he chose to fuck with his own flesh and blood. I just don't get why he wouldn't try to connect with me. I'm a state trooper. He could have tried to put me on his payroll."

"Would you have gone for that?" Jared asked.

"You've got to be fucking kidding me. I can't believe you'd even ask me that question."

"Just doing my due diligence."

Reese glanced at his watch. Stacey must be enjoying herself, since she was the trooper that got to go along for the arrest. Frank and Reese were too personal with the case, and Jared wasn't even on duty. Reese wasn't worried about how green Stacey was because he trusted her with his life, but so far, nothing. Until Stacey barreled through the doors.

"He's gone," she said. "The task force was in place. Had all the proper warrants. Everything was perfect, except it took too long."

"What the fuck happened?" Reese asked. "We've had tails on him for days."

"He had a dummy car," Stacey said. "When we arrived at his hotel, his SUV was in the lot. We ran the plates. It was his. We stormed the room. Nothing. Just gone."

"Conrad?" Frank asked.

"Oh, we got him, and he and his family are in a safe house. FBI and State's Attorney already copped a deal with him. He won't see any jail time, but the poor bastard won't be able to practice law."

Reese called Patty but got voicemail. Same with Nana. "Fuck."

"What is it?" Stacey asked. "I don't like your tone."

"Can't get a hold of Patty or Nana."

"I drove by. Cars in the driveway. It all looked good. I'll call my dad and Doug. They'll go over and check on them."

"I'll go," Reese said as he started to gather his belongings.

"Holland had to have known he showed his hand and we connected the dots with you being his son." Stacey shook her head.

"He did," said a familiar voice from behind Reese. He so didn't want to turn around because he knew exactly who that voice belonged to.

"Who are you?" Stacey asked.

"I think that's his wife," Frank said sarcastically.

"I heard you were looking for me," Jessica said.

Reese opened his mouth to say something, but nothing came out. He cleared his throat. "Your timing is interesting."

"Not really." Jessica waltzed across the room, her long red hair flowing as if she were a model in the middle of a shoot. She wore cowboy boots, skinny jeans, a tight shirt showing off her cleavage, and a lined jean jacket. A far cry from the country club girl he thought he'd met.

She got so close he had to take a step back. He felt every single eye in the station on him. Or her. Or both. He was grateful for that because, had it been anywhere else, his response to her might have been deadly.

"What? No hug and kiss for your long-lost wife?"

"Unless that envelope in your hands is divorce papers, you and I don't have much to say."

"That would make you happy, now, wouldn't it?" She handed him the envelope, but not before leaning in close and whispering in his ear. "I guess you didn't know, I work for Holland. Holland is not only going to destroy you, but he's going to get his revenge, and all your money, and finally, I will get a piece of the pie. Your meddling grandmother and that nasty little girlfriend are alive, but not for long, so I suggest you do as instructed without letting anyone in this room know."

He took the envelope, glancing Stacey's way. He had only seconds to catch her gaze and pray they had that secret language.

"Perhaps we can take this outside, where it's a bit more private?" Jessica whispered.

Reese glanced inside the envelope, and it was all he could do to keep from vomiting. "Sure thing." He wrapped his hand around Jessica's bicep and squeezed as hard as he could. He knew he bruised her, and to her credit, she pretended he wasn't hurting her until they got outside.

"Get your fucking hands off me." She managed to escape his grip. "They are going to die unless I get you there, right quick. So, I suggest you get in the car and shut the fuck up." She pulled back her coat, showing a weapon. "And trust me when I say I don't care if they live or die. I'm only in this for the money. The money I deserve, after marrying you and then being abandoned."

"Abandoned? That's funny."

"You drive," she said, ignoring his jab.

He got in the front seat and turned the key and punched the gas. As he followed her directions, with a gun pointed at his side, he continued to glance in the rearview mirror, but saw no sign of Stacey. Or Frank. Or Jared.

But he hoped they were somewhere behind him.

"I'm so sorry. This is all my fault," Nana said.

Patty didn't blame anyone but Keith Holland for her current predicament. "We need to focus on how to get out of here."

"We need to find a way to untie ourselves."

"That's pretty hard without a knife," Patty said. She was duct-taped to a chair in an abandoned warehouse with the great-grandmother of her child, and she was sure they were both about to die at the hands of her baby's grandfather. Talk about a mindfuck. This predicament actually called for a few cuss words.

"Elizabeth," Holland said as he stepped from the shadows. "We have some business to discuss."

"You won't get away with this. The cops are onto you."

"I'm not worried about a few cops," he said. "Including my stupid son. So disappointing to see he's so much like his mother."

"You're a bastard," Nana said.

"True," Holland said. "But your husband was just as bad. How long has it been since he passed? Two years?"

"Don't you ever speak of my husband."

Patty couldn't stand to listen. She chose instead to focus on trying to free her hands, but it seemed useless. She glanced at Nana, then to Holland. "What do you want with us?"

Holland laughed. "What I've always wanted. The Baxter fortune."

Patty was about to say not as long as she were alive, but she realized he had no intention of keeping them alive, and whatever he had planned, it wouldn't be pinned on him.

"We gave you plenty." Nana struggled to break free but failed miserably.

Holland nodded. "You gave me a good start, but your husband continued to fund me, so when he died, and those payments stopped—"

"You're lying!" Nana lurched, knocking her chair over, smacking the side of her head on the cement floor with a loud thud. She cried out in pain.

"Someone lift this old woman up," Holland said, and one of his cronies scooped her up, setting her upright. The side of her cheek was already bruised and swollen. A bit of blood dripped from her mouth.

"Now, how is it that a smart woman like you didn't know your husband paid me every year to keep me quiet and out of my son's life?"

"He's not your son." Nana's voice trembled. Patty could tell she was a bit dazed and confused from the knock on the head.

Patty looked around, trying to count the men in the room. She saw four, including Holland. Doors on both ends of the building and skylights above. There were options, if she could get herself untied, but she would get her and her baby killed trying to escape. And to think, last summer, she had said she wanted more excitement in her life.

"Biology doesn't lie," Holland said, waving his gun around as he circled them like a shark. "I always thought it would be nice to get to know Reese. What a horrible name. Whose idea was that?" He paused, waving his gun in Nana's face. "I often dreamed of bringing him into my business. Teaching him, so one day he could take it over."

"I seriously doubt that."

Holland backhanded Nana.

"Leave her alone," Patty said behind gritted teeth.

Holland waved his gun in her direction. "I'd shut up if I were you. Now, where was I? Oh, yes. My son. See, I did have those thoughts, but God, I did not want anything to do with that batshit crazy daughter of yours. About the only thing she was good at was giving blow jobs, and even those got boring."

"You're a disgusting pig," Nana said.

Holland stood over Nana, his gun to her temple. "Eleanor came to me after Reese was born. I refused to see her, but I did sneak a peek at my boy, and I knew he was mine. I thought for a moment I might want him. I actually went to your husband, but Alistair refused to turn the boy over to me. Ultimately, I'm a greedy man, so when he offered me more money to stay out of the kid's life, I milked that until the bastard up and died. I thought that he would have made a provision for those payments to continue, but he did not. So, I thought I'd come find my son and see what he was doing."

"You knew all along that he was here?" Patty asked.

"I've always known where my son was." He tugged at Nana's hair. "See, he wasn't supposed to shoot Terry. I could have gotten Terry off easily that day. I just wanted to see my son in action. Boy, did I see him. Good shot. Takes after his father that way. I also knew he was too brainwashed by you and Alistair. So, I had to get rid of him."

"You've a very cruel man," Patty said. "Please, let Elizabeth be. For now, your gripe is with me and Reese."

"I don't think so." Holland shrugged. "Now, Elizabeth. You start making those payments again, and we can call it even."

"The cops are going to be here soon," Nana said.

"Yeah, I sort of showed my ass, didn't I?" Holland let Nana's hair go, then inched closer to Patty. "But I'm not worried, because Elizabeth is going to give me all her money, and then I'll just disappear."

"Over my dead body," Nana said.

"No," Holland said. "Over Patty's and her baby's dead bodies."

Reese pulled into the abandoned parking lot of the old Kendrick Paper Company. Almost nothing remained to indicate this property had been a business.

"Why?" he asked as he walked with Jessica toward the deserted building.

"Why, what?"

"The abortion?"

"There was never supposed to be a baby. Holland paid me to marry you. Not have your kid. I didn't want it, so I got rid of it. I never anticipated your nana would find out."

"Did you get pregnant on purpose?"

She laughed. "No, but it served a purpose. It got you to marry me. Holland thought I should keep the baby, but no way was I going to do that. I figured I'd pretend to have a miscarriage, but that didn't work out. So when you took off, Holland let me go. That sucked, until about a year ago, when he saw you settling down with some woman, so he decided to pay me to see what you were up to. I've been staked out in this godforsaken place for months."

"Please, no. I'll do whatever you want," he heard Nana say, her voice weak and trembling. He assessed the situation, wondering how far behind the cavalry was, and how long would it take them to figure out a plan.

The warehouse was empty, other than some junk and a few empty beer cans left behind by teenagers looking for a place to party on weekends.

"You're a cold and sad woman." Reese followed Jessica through the doors, then around the corner, where he saw Nana and Patty tied to chairs. They saw him as soon as he entered the room.

"I don't care what you think," Jessica said. "Package delivered," she said to Holland.

"Oh, a little family reunion," Holland said. "Patty, have you met Reese's wife?"

"Can I have my money, please?" Jessica asked. "And then I'll be on my way."

"I can see why you don't want to be with this

one," Holland said to Reese. "Whiny little bitch...and the answer is no. Not yet. So go stand over there."

Reese tried not to focus on how banged-up Nana was, and instead attempted to figure out a plan to get them out of this intact. "What do you want, Holland?"

"Money," he said. "It's always about money."

A man with a briefcase and a laptop appeared. Someone else set up a folding table, then placed it in front of Nana. "This here," Holland said, taking a stack of papers from the man, "is your new will. Well, not new, since it's backdated two years. Sign it."

He shoved a pen in her face.

Reese wanted to tell her to do everything extra slow, but it looked like she'd already figured that out as he hand shook with every broad stroke she made. Reese glanced at Patty, who locked gazes with him immediately. The love pouring out of her was over-whelming. His knees nearly buckled, but he broke the gaze and went back to the impossible situation.

"Good girl," Holland said. "Now, access your bank accounts, and transfer all your cash assets into this account." He opened the laptop and gave Nana a piece of paper. "This is for Jessica's trouble." Once again, she did as instructed. The only noises were her fingers tapping the keyboard and a few swallowed sobs.

"It's been a real pleasure," Holland said. "Time to make this look like a crazy, unfortunate accident."

"Impossible," Reese said. "Conrad rolled over on you. He confessed everything about how you've been blackmailing him, getting him to break the law for you."

"He'll redact it once you're out of the picture," Holland said. "He won't have a choice."

"You'll kill your own son," Nana said. "Your grandson. Just for money?"

"Of course." Holland shrugged. "Should have thought about that when you blackmailed me for something I didn't do. Your daughter practically begged me to take her innocence."

Reese heard activity from outside.

The Calvary had finally arrived. He closed his eyes and clenched his hands. "I'm going to be the one killing you," he said.

Holland laughed. "Doubtful."

"You'll at least be behind bars and I'll get my divorce from your lackey," he said. He didn't get a chance to finish his redirect before the first kill shot came through the skylight, hitting Holland square in the chest. Reese pulled his gun, something Jessica hadn't thought to look for and nailed two of the other men, who were heading for the doors. He turned to Jessica as she bolted toward the exit. "I'd stop if I were you."

"Nope," she yelled. "You'll have to shoot me in the back."

Before Reese could pull the trigger, the doors swung open. Jessica fired a shot and two more rang out. Jessica dropped to the floor. Reese raced back to Nana and Patty, trying to untie them both at the same time and failing miserably.

"Let me help," Stacey said, taking over untying Nana.

He nodded and turned to Patty. "Are you hurt?"

She shook her head.

"Nana? How you doing?" he asked.

"Been worse," she said.

Reese would never be able to truly piece together the next moments in coherent thought. Holland, his biological father was dead. Despite his mother's insanity and addiction, and his grandparents' lies, they had all tried to protect him from a very bad man.

And in many ways, they had succeeded.

That counted for something.

Then there was Jessica. As she lay there, dying in

Jared's arms, she refused to admit to anything. Her last words were 'Fuck off.' The only resolution she left Reese was that he was now a free man. Free to start a life with the woman of his dreams.

Nana apologized profusely for keeping her knowledge of his father from him, and he understood her motives. He probably would have done the same thing in the same situation. In the end, as they loaded Nana into the ambulance, she told him the fortune was his, to do with what he saw appropriate, as long as he took good care of Patty, his child, and of course, his nana.

He held his nana's hand and kissed it. "I should ride with you."

"No. You need to stay with Patty," Nana said.

"I'll stay with her," Stacey said as she climbed into the ambulance. "I don't mind."

"Thanks." The question was, how much of it did he want? Money seemed to do weird things to people. All he wanted was to provide a good stable home for his family. I didn't need the whole ball of wax.

Just enough to ensure The Heritage Inn would provide a positive legacy for *his* family.

He understood now why his grandparents made it so hard for him. Made him pay his own way. They had seen, firsthand, what true greed did to a person.

Themselves included.

It wasn't pretty.

"I'm riding with her," he said to the other ambulance tech as they loaded Patty into the vehicle.

"I'm fine," Patty protested. "You can ride with Nana."

"If I don't ride with you, my nana will toss me over her knee like a small child. No one wants to see her do that.." He climbed into the ambulance. "Two heartbeats?" he asked.

"Yes, sir," the EMT said. "Both, nice and strong."

"Huh, I won't be needing..." He shook his head. He never wished Jessica dead. There was no love lost, but she was still human.

"Needing what?" Patty asked.

"A divorce," he whispered.

"That's kind of cold," Patty said.

"That's weird, coming from someone who was tied up partly because of that woman."

"True." Patty gripped his hand tighter. "Still, seems rather crass of us to be thinking what I know we are both thinking."

He nodded. There was a time and a place for everything. "I love you," he said.

"I know."

"One thing at a time." He sat down next to the woman he couldn't live without, holding her hand as the sirens blared and the ambulance inched out of the parking lot. They had their whole lives ahead of them.

Epilogue

Reese leaned against a post on the front porch of the residency. The sun had started to set, but did nothing for the humidity that came with the month of June. Reese hardly noticed as he sipped his beer and loosened his tie. The last few months had been a blur, and he had yet to process it all. His biological father was dead. His first wife. Dead. Death seemed to loom over his head like a rash that wouldn't go away.

At the same time, those deaths had a different purpose. Holland wasn't a nice guy, and he now understood what his mother had meant. Why she'd lied about Allen. In her final days, her mind had been destroyed by the cancer. She often spoke of strange things. But her last words had come from a moment of caring and wanting to stop the lies.

"It was a nice ceremony," Frank said, leaning on another post, sipping his beer and looking out at the lake. "Still can't believe you did it."

"I can't believe you agreed to be my best man."

"Lacy would have strung me out to dry if I had refused." Frank pulled up one of the big rocking chairs. "Especially since she and your nana spent the last month putting this wedding together."

Reese pulled up a chair as well. He fiddled with his wedding ring. "I've never felt like this before."

"Like what?" Frank asked.

"Like I fit in somewhere. I went from one military tour to the next. One job to the next, never feeling like I was part of what I was doing. Until I got here. It started before Patty, but she has been the key. Like my entire life was leading up to being right here, right now."

Reese heard Patty giggle. "I married a sentimental sap."

"Yeah, you did." Reese wiped his eyes, then patted his legs. His smiling bride sat on his lap, wrapping her arm around his shoulder, while he managed to rest his hand on her slightly bulging belly. Patty said she felt the baby move all the time.

So far Reese had felt it only a few times, so every opportunity he got, his hand rested on her stomach, waiting to connect with his unborn child.

Lacy, in turn, settled herself on Frank's lap.

"Well, now, that sure is cute," Stacey said as she stepped onto the porch. "I'm happy for you, but it's so gonna suck without you at the station."

Reese had to admit he would miss being a cop, but he didn't regret his decision to retire and run the inn full time with his wife and Nana. Truly a family business. A legacy he could be proud of. "Yeah, have fun working with no-sense-of-humor Frank."

"I'm funny."

Even Lacy laughed at that. "You're uptight and serious."

"Thanks for defending me," Frank said.

"I've got to hit the road," Stacey said. "On duty and all, and Jared keeps giving me the evil eye."

"Glad you were able to come," Patty said. "I appreciate everything you've done for us."

"Not much could have kept me from seeing that old man get married."

Andy rushed past Stacey, chasing a couple of Jared's toddlers, and Jake, Frank's younger brother, ran behind him. "Sorry. No one ever told me babysitting would be so exhausting." Andy caught one of the toddlers, and Jake caught the other. "I need a nap." Andy hiked back up the stairs and into the residency.

Jared and his wife joined everyone on the porch.

"You ready for all of that?" Jared asked. "Because it's like that every day."

"You only know the half of it," Ryan said. "And want to see me make Jared's face get all contorted and weird-looking?"

"Ryan, don't even joke about stuff like that." Jared's face only half contorted.

"Not joking. The rabbit died."

"Must be something in the water," Lacy said. "Because our rabbit died, too."

"What?" Frank's face lit up like Christmas. "You said you were going to wait to take the test."

Lacy shrugged. "I waited until you left the room."

"It's going to be a lot of fun around here in a few months," Patty said. "Reese?"

"Is he crying?" Stacey asked.

"Just got something in my eye." Reese used his sleeve to wipe the few tears away, but it was no use. At least they were happy tears.

"He's been like this for days," Patty said. "When I asked to see a softer side of Reese, I sure got what I asked for. Congratulations to all the pregos. May you always see your feet."

"Yeah, good luck with that," Ryan said.

"Stacey," Jared barked. "You best get back on the road."

"Yes, sir."

"And," Jared said. "You did real good with wrapping up this case. I know that was tough on you, right after it all went down, but you did what you were trained to do." He handed her a twenty. "I did change your diapers."

"Now that you say it, it's kind of gross and creepy," Stacey said.

Everyone laughed, but Reese, who was barely listening. He tilted his bride's face. "I want this. All of this. The chaos of kids. The crazy of normal family. People in and out. Sitting on the front porch, watching the sunset, and loving you. I love you, and I'm never letting go."

"Better hold on tight because being married to me is going to be one hell of a ride."

Thank you for taking the time to read *Deadly Secrets*. Next up in the *NY State Trooper Series* is **Murder in Paradise Bay**. This is Doug and Stacey's story. I'm super excited to share their long-awaited romance with you! Please don't forget to leave an HONEST review wherever you happened to purchase your copy of this book.

Don't forget to check out the *First Responder Series*, in which many of the NY State Trooper gang often makes an appearance as well as the *Legacy Series* and the *Love in the Adirondack Series*. Doug makes a special appearance in **THE WEDDING DRIVER.**

Check out LOVE IN THE ADIRONDACKS!
AN INCONVENIENT FLAME
SHATTERED DREAMS
THE WEDDING DRIVER
CLEAR BLUE SKY

A spin-off from the NY State Troopers series
PLAYING WITH FIRE
PRIVATE CONVERSATION
THE RIGHT GROOM
AFTER THE FIRE
CAUGHT IN THE FLAMES
CHASING THE FIRE

Legacy Series

Dark Legacy
Legacy of Lies
Secret Legacy

Sign up for my Newsletter where I often give away free books before publication.

Join my private Facebook group where she posts exclusive excerpts and discuss all things murder and love!

About the Author

Jen Talty is a USA Today Bestselling Author of Contemporary Romance, Romantic Suspense, and Paranormal Romance. In the fall of 2020, a short story of hers was selected and featured in a 1001 Dark Knights Anthology. She is currently contracted to write in the _With Me_ series by Kristen Proby with Lady Boss Press as well as Susan Stoker's _Special Forces: Operation Alpha_ and Elle James's _Brotherhood Protectors_.

Regardless of the genre, her goal is to take you on a ride that will leave you floating under the sun with warmth in your heart. She writes stories about broken heroes and heroines who aren't necessarily looking for romance, but in the end, they find the kind of love books are written about :).

She first started writing while carting her kids to one hockey rink after the other, averaging 170 games per year between 3 kids in 2 countries and 5 states. Her first book, IN TWO WEEKS was originally published in 2007. In 2010 she helped form a publishing company (Cool Gus Publishing) with NY Times Bestselling Author Bob Mayer where she ran the technical side of the business through 2016.

Jen is currently enjoying the next phase of her life… the empty NESTER! She and her husband reside in Jupiter, Florida.

Grab a glass of vino, kick back, relax, and let the romance roll in…

Sign up for my [Newsletter](https://dl.bookfunnel.com/6atcf7g1be) where I often give away free books before publication.

Join my private [Facebook group](https://www.facebook.com/groups/191706547909047/) where I post exclusive excerpts and discuss all things murder and love!

And on Bookbub: bookbub.com/authors/jen-talty

facebook.com/AuthorJenTalty

instagram.com/jen_talty

bookbub.com/authors/jen-talty

amazon.com/author/jentalty

pinterest.com/jentalty

Also by Jen Talty

Brand new series: SAFE HARBOR!

MINE TO KEEP

MINE TO SAVE

MINE TO PROTECT

Check out LOVE IN THE ADIRONDACKS!

AN INCONVENIENT FLAME

SHATTERED DREAMS

THE WEDDING DRIVER

CLEAR BLUE SKY

NY STATE TROOPER SERIES (also set in the Adirondacks!)

In Two Weeks

Dark Water

Deadly Secrets

Murder in Paradise Bay

To Protect His own

Deadly Seduction

When A Stranger Calls

His Deadly Past

The Corkscrew Killer

Brand New Novella for the First Responders series

A spin-off from the NY State Troopers series

PLAYING WITH FIRE

PRIVATE CONVERSATION

THE RIGHT GROOM

AFTER THE FIRE

CAUGHT IN THE FLAMES

CHASING THE FIRE

Legacy Series

Dark Legacy

Legacy of Lies

Secret Legacy

Emerald City

INVESTIGATE AWAY

SAIL AWAY

Colorado Brotherhood Protectors

Fighting For Esme

Defending Raven

Fay's Six

Yellowstone Brotherhood Protectors

Guarding Payton

Candlewood Falls

RIVERS EDGE

THE BURIED SECRET

ITS IN HIS KISS

LIPS OF AN ANGEL

It's all in the Whiskey

JOHNNIE WALKER

GEORGIA MOON

JACK DANIELS

JIM BEAM

WHISKEY SOUR

WHISKEY COBBLER

WHISKEY SMASH

IRISH WHISKEY

The Monroes

COLOR ME YOURS

COLOR ME SMART

COLOR ME FREE

COLOR ME LUCKY

COLOR ME ICE

COLOR ME HOME

Search and Rescue

PROTECTING AINSLEY

PROTECTING CLOVER

PROTECTING OLYMPIA

PROTECTING FREEDOM

PROTECTING PRINCESS

PROTECTING MARLOWE

DELTA FORCE-NEXT GENERATION

SHIELDING JOLENE

SHIELDING AALYIAH

SHIELDING LAINE

SHIELDING TALULLAH

SHIELDING MARIBEL

The Men of Thief Lake

REKINDLED

DESTINY'S DREAM

BURNING BED

REMEMBER ME ALWAYS

The Brotherhood Protectors

Out of the Wild

ROUGH JUSTICE

ROUGH AROUND THE EDGES

ROUGH RIDE

ROUGH EDGE

ROUGH BEAUTY

The Brotherhood Protectors

The Saving Series

SAVING LOVE

SAVING MAGNOLIA

SAVING LEATHER

Hot Hunks

Cove's Blind Date Blows Up

My Everyday Hero – Ledger

Tempting Tavor

Malachi's Mystic Assignment

Needing Neor

www.ingramcontent.com/pod-product-compliance
Lightning Source LLC
Chambersburg PA
CBHW010734130726
47899CB00015B/3256